"We have word, sir," Adams called out. "She has been found."

He turned in the cold mist. He was old. All these years he had waited, and now it was time.

"And will she come?"

"She will come, sir," Adams said. "I will make certain that she comes to Ravenshurst."

A millionaire and a million-dollar whore, a star-maker and a nation-killer, a woman whose lusts were as cold as graveyard snow . . . Five of the most powerful people in the world, gathered in an ancient mansion to inherit a Legacy of bloodsome horror. And Maggie makes six.

THE LEGACY

THE LEGACY

KATHARINE ROSS   SAM ELLIOTT

ARNOLD KOPELSON Presents A TURMAN-FOSTER Production

Co-Starring ROGER DALTREY

Music by MICHAEL J. LEWIS

Screenplay by JIMMY SANGSTER, PATRICK TILLEY and PAUL WHEELER

Story by JIMMY SANGSTER

Associate Producer: TED LLOYD

Executive Producer: ARNOLD KOPELSON

Produced by DAVID FOSTER

Directed by RICHARD MARQUAND

"Another Side of Me," Sung by KIKI DEE

A UNIVERSAL RELEASE

A PETHURST LTD. PRODUCTION

The Legacy

A NOVEL BY JOHN COYNE

BASED ON A STORY
BY JIMMY SANGSTER

A BERKLEY BOOK
published by
BERKLEY PUBLISHING CORPORATION

THE LEGACY

A Berkley Book / published by arrangement with
MCA PUBLISHING, A Division of MCA, Inc.

PRINTING HISTORY
Berkley edition / April 1979
8 printings through September 1979
NINTH PRINTING

ISBN: 0-425-04183-2

A BERKLEY BOOK ® TM 757,375
Berkley Books are published by Berkley Publishing Corporation,
200 Madison Avenue, New York, New York 10016.

PRINTED IN THE UNITED STATES OF AMERICA

To Tom Hebert,
who loves a conspiracy

The Legacy

Prologue

AT DUSK HE BECAME RESTLESS, for the night always troubled him. He would leave his rooms to roam the hallways of the old stone mansion, turning on lights as he walked through the empty estate. Occasionally travelers, lost on these ancient roads that ran down to the sea, would pass the manor house high on the hillside and see the lights blazing like a wildfire.

If they could stop a local person on the road, they'd ask the way, and inquire about the lighted mansion. And if the local people would talk, they'd say it was only the master, awake as always. He hated the night, they'd whisper, as his mother had hated it before him. She would burn candles the length of the night, it was told, in a frantic attempt to hold back the creeping darkness. And he was his mother's child.

He left the rooms of the north wing, the rooms where his mother had once lived, where he had lived since childhood, and went through the Portrait Hall, passing the old paintings of his family, all the ancestors, his uncles and aunts and distant cousins.

Often he spent hours here among these lost relations, remembering when his family had gathered in these rooms and numbered in the hundreds. Now he was the only one left in these ancient halls.

Tonight, though, he passed through the Portrait Hall without stopping, his footsteps echoing on the hardwood floors of the sixteenth-century building. Tonight he waited for the end of his long search and he would not sleep until word was received. Even the small white household cat sensed his anxiety and raced ahead, a flash of white in the dark halls, as it led the way to the library, to the last portrait of his mother.

And there before the fireplace he sat in a deep leather chair, holding the small cat in his arms, and looked up at his mother's painting, thinking of her days of glory, when kings and queens paid homage to her beauty and feared her wealth and power.

By dawn, when word still had not come, he went out of the house. Fog rolled across the land and broke on the gray stone walls of the mansion. It had settled on the river below, then slowly filled the trees of the small forest and finally, with the daylight, spread across the fields, a cold, fathomless cloud.

He stood in the mist looking toward the horizon,

toward the sun, but it was not warmth he sought. He had followed the seasons for too many years, and another brilliant sunrise held no surprise or pleasure. He had seen it all, done it all, been it all.

All these years since his mother's death, he had waited for the sun only so that he might have another day to continue his mission. And now he was very close to the end. The time had come for the one blood heir to be put to the test.

He turned toward the great Elizabethan mansion and saw Adams approaching.

"We have word, sir," Adams called out.

He sighed, as if he were allowing the life to drain out of him. Then he looked at Adams and gave his orders.

"We must convene this weekend. There won't be much time, now."

"Yes, sir. I know where they are."

"Karl then?"

"In Ethiopia, sir. He left yesterday from Frankfurt. I have his hotel in Addis Ababa."

"And the others?"

"Mr. Jackson is in America. Miss Kirstenburg is in Paris. She is preparing her new collection. Miss Gabrielli is, of course, in Rome. Mr. Grandier is in the south of Spain."

He nodded. "Very good, Adams. Let everyone know immediately." He moved toward the mansion. It would not be long now, and as if the servant could read his thoughts, Adams said:

"Your room has been prepared, sir."

"Thank you, Adams. Thank you for everything." At the entrance of the mansion he stopped, weary from the long night, from his long search, and said thoughtfully, "We will soon see, Adams, if the bloodline of my ancestors is more powerful than the greed and cunning of the creatures I have raised up."

"I have no doubt, sir," Adams answered quickly.

"We have waited a long time, haven't we, Adams?" He smiled fondly at his servant.

"Yes, sir. But you always knew that in time..."

He nodded. "Have you reached her, Adams?"

"Not yet, sir, but I will."

"And will she come?" he asked insistently.

Adams hesitated a moment, then replied calmly, "She will come, sir. I will make certain that she comes to Ravenshurst."

Chapter One

IT WAS MAGGIE THEY REALLY WANTED.

The telegram from London reached southern California late on Monday afternoon and she read it as she walked through the house to their studio off the sun porch.

"Pete, you're not going to believe this!" she announced, coming into the bright, white room.

He looked up from his architect's desk and frowned, unsure of what she had said. He had been engrossed in his drawings and immediately he was angry. She knew better than to interrupt when he was working. It was their cardinal rule for sharing space.

"Maggie, come on!" He shoved his stool away from the high desk. "I'll never get these damn plans done!"

"Read this," she continued, ignoring his anger, and tossed the telegram onto his desk. Her hazel eyes flashed. She wasn't someone who could conceal her pleasure.

He leaned forward and scanned the small sheet of paper. Then he seized it to read carefully, a smile spreading across his face.

REQUEST MAGGIE WALSH OF DANNER/
WALSH ASSOCIATES TO DESIGN AND
FURNISH NEW GRANDIER LIMITED OFFICE
COMPLEX TOTTENHAM COURT ROAD LON-
DON. FIFTY THOUSAND DOLLARS ADVANCE
FOR PRELIMINARY EXPENSES AND FIRST
CLASS PLANE TICKET BEING POSTED REG-
ISTERED MAIL. CABLE ETA HEATHROW.

GRANDIER

Pete looked up at Maggie. "But why you?"

She shrugged and grinned. "Maybe they saw that article in *Designers West*. It said I was the best new interior designer in Los Angeles."

"Maggie, this is an office complex on Tottenham Court Road, London, England. This is a job for someone like Welton Beck. You're good, but you're still a small-time California designer. You're not in the same league as, say, Jim Wood. And he has London experience."

"Maybe they want us because we're less expensive. We don't have such big overhead."

"Believe me, these guys aren't worried about saving a few hundred pounds on an interior designer. They're sending you ten thousand dollars. Isn't that a bit grandiose if they're trying to cut corners?"

"Oh, Pete, what difference does it make? They want us, okay? Isn't that enough of an explanation? And they're even giving us expense money up front. That's more than we can say about most of our clients."

Pete sighed. He would have a hard time making her reconsider. When she decided what she wanted, she wouldn't listen to reason. "What about Crichton's house?" he asked.

"Oh, *no!*" She spun away from the desk and paced the room, her hands wedged into the back pockets of her tight cut-off jeans. The March afternoon was chilly, but she wore only a pair of cut-offs that hugged her bottom and a tight tan T-shirt with UPPITY WOMEN UNITE printed across the front. Even from across the room Peter could see where the dark nipples pressed against the cotton.

"How about doing it this way?" she said, still pacing. "We'll telegram England saying we'll arrive on Monday morning. Then we'll work all night tonight and tomorrow on Crichton's plans and sketches and give them to him on Wednesday afternoon. We can take the night flight over the pole to London and that will give us four days on our own before we have to start." She paused and looked at Peter, waiting for him to agree with her.

He shook his head. "Look at the telegram,

Maggie. It's not *we* they want; it's *you*: Maggie Walsh of Danner/Walsh Associates." He picked up the telegram to show her, but she backed off.

"Oh, no, I'm not going alone. I never bummed around England like you did. I've never even been to a foreign country."

"It's okay; they speak English."

"That's not the point!" she flared. "It won't be any fun without you. Look, we'll go together, have four days in the country, and maybe a few more days in London while I make some initial sketches. Then you can fly home and I'll stay on and finish the job." She came up behind him and linked her arms around his neck. "Besides, we're a team, Pete, aren't we?" She nuzzled closer and kissed his neck.

"Don't, Maggie." He tried to shake her off, but she wouldn't let go. He knew she was an outrageous flirt when she wanted something, but still he couldn't resist.

"The Crichton house," he started to say, but she shook her head and kissed him. He put his hands on her waist and pushed her away.

"Damn it, Maggie, listen! This Crichton job is important to me; it's important to *us*. If we do a good job, and people like what they see, it means more work in the desert."

"Pete, this is a trip to England. We could have such a good time. We could go look for my ancestral home." She smiled and tried to catch his eyes, but he kept shaking his head. She always distracted him when she looked at her. She had that elementary power over him.

"We can't just bag Crichton. The office complex job is nice for you—lots of quick money, a free trip to England. But our future, your future, is in Los Angeles!"

He had worked himself up lecturing to her. She just didn't have business sense. It ticked him off at times, but he knew she had a surer sense of how to design a room or furnish a house than almost anyone else, and he knew she knew it. She also knew that he was in love with her and would put up with all her petulant ways.

Still . . .

"Maggie, we can't delay any longer. Crichton won't wait forever, and we're already late. You haven't even started on the sketches."

"That's because he keeps changing his mind!" She pulled away and paced the room. It was a few moments before she spoke. "We need a vacation. We haven't been anywhere in over a year." She glanced at him. "All I'm suggesting is one crummy week." There were tears in her eyes. "Don't we owe something to ourselves, Pete? To our relationship?"

Pete tossed down his pen. Then he slid off the chair and went to her. She was at it again: acting bitchy, put-upon, deprived. All that insecurity. Now he would have to calm her, pull her back from the edge of a crying jag. He had practice, and he knew how to handle her.

First he held her. He slipped his hand behind her head and eased her head onto his shoulder. His other arm he wrapped around her waist and moved her body tight against him, locking her so she couldn't move.

In a few moments she relaxed and her body moved closer to him, settling against his strength. It was a curious reaction, but the display of his strength always made her relax. She lacked self-assurance; he gave her confidence and strength. It was as if, despite her talent and charm, she were missing something—as if she were incomplete in some way.

She let him hold her. She loved the feeling of being safe in his arms; she could stay that way for hours. Then she felt his arms tighten, and he pressed against her.

"Pete, you just finished telling me about all the work we have to do."

"Oh, come on," he urged, smoothing his hands over her shoulders and back.

"I thought we were going to work all night."

"This will only take a few minutes, and besides," he added, "you won't be so grumpy afterwards."

Reluctantly she raised her arms and Pete reached for her T-shirt, pulling it up and off her body. Then he lifted her in his arms and together they settled on the cushions beneath the room's high skylight, where the winter sun warmed a patch of bright blue fabric.

For a few moments they stretched out on the warm cushions, not embracing, but watching each other's bodies. Maggie never grew tired of looking at him. He was very dark. Brownish-black hair and eyebrows, and dark eyes the color of sable. And he had grown a thick mustache. He looked menacing, but she knew he wasn't. She never had known anyone so nice, and no one in her whole crazy life had ever been kinder to her. He had kept her sane, helped her get her life straightened out, and given her a chance at a real career. She would always love him for those reasons alone.

She leaned slightly forward and kissed his chest,

and he took her in his arms. They were silent now, purposeful, and they made love as if it were the most important thing in the world. He caught a glimpse of their bodies in the mirror, his almost concealing hers. She had such a beautiful body, he thought, but somehow he felt her resistance was growing instead of melting. There had always been a core of resistance he could never get through; it would arise suddenly, inexplicably. Her passion would cool. That was how it had been lately.

She embraced him even more tightly, but he knew. He always did.

"What is it?" He moved back a little so he could see her eyes.

Before she could answer, the telephone rang. He tried to hold her eyes, but the ringing continued, insistently, and Maggie slipped away to answer it. It was Crichton's secretary.

"Oh, my God!" Maggie cried, clutching the receiver. "Oh, the poor man." She listened a few more minutes and then hung up, saying quietly to Pete, "Crichton is dead. His secretary said it was a coronary. He was taking a sauna at his club and they found him lying against the door. Evidently he was trying to get out, but the door had jammed."

Pete lay on his back for a moment, staring up at the skylight. Then he got up and walked to his desk and began to roll up his blueprints. "Well, it solves your problem," he said.

"What?"

"There's nothing keeping you from London. You're free of work, and we can use the job." He grimaced. "No one is going to build Crichton's dream house."

"I won't go unless you do, Pete." She stepped

around the desk, her eyes pleading for him to say yes. "We're a team, remember—work together, play together." She nuzzled him.

Pete sighed. She was right; there really was no reason not to go to London now. "You always get your way, don't you, Maggie Walsh?" he said.

Chapter Two

From the window of their room in the wonderful old Victorian Hyde Park Hotel, Maggie could see Kensington Garden, the acres of green lawn that made so much of London seem like a country estate. It had been raining when they arrived at Heathrow, but now the sun had come out. It glistened off the wet foliage of the Garden and the icy blue water of Serpentine Lake.

It was a weak winter sun, though, and Maggie was freezing as she stood barefoot at the window with a blanket wrapped around her. The steam heat of the old hotel hissed and clanked, but it could not keep her warm. She had been born and raised in

California, and the damp cold of London chilled her to the bone.

"Come here," Pete said, rolling over in the bed, the fresh white sheets rustling as he moved. They had come in from the airport and gone immediately to bed, exhausted from the overnight flight.

"I can't, I'm too hyper." Maggie glanced around, her face beaming. "Isn't it exciting being in a foreign country?"

Pete smiled at her pleasure. He had fallen in love with London during the year he studied city planning at the London School of Economics. The great buildings of Europe had convinced him to give up city planning for architecture. Now he wanted Maggie to see London, and share her pleasure at discovering its treasures: Marble Hill House, Southwark Cathedral, Cheyne Walk, and the houses around Regents Park.

He sat up and threw off the sheets and blankets. "Maggie, let's get dressed. I was thinking we should try and see..."

She turned away from the windows and interrupted. "Pete, could we go by Tottenham Court Road first and look at the office building?"

"But you don't want Grandier to know you're in London."

"They won't have to know who we are. Now that I'm here, I'd like to get an idea of the space I have to work with."

She came back to sit beside him on the bed, looking submissive, as if her whole life was subject to his whims and wants. It was her usual behavior when she wanted something, and it always worked.

"Sure." He kissed her lightly, happy to please

her. "I'll check the address in the phone book and we'll case the joint."

Fitzroy Square was dominated by office buildings, but Grandier Limited was immediately obvious. It was a glass and steel structure that shot up like a silver bullet, towering over the other offices, its top floors disappearing completely into the London fog. Pete pushed open the glass doors and they went dripping wet into the Italian blue marble lobby. In the center a small fountain bubbled, the water spurting through the iron ribs of an abstract sculpture.

"It's a Montesi!" Maggie exclaimed, peering closely at the signature hammered into the metal base. "I never expected to find an avant-garde Italian in an English office building."

"At least you know one thing," Pete commented. "They're not going to want you to redesign this lobby. I wonder what Grandier Limited does to afford this museum piece."

The building's directory had the answer. There were Grandier Holiday Villas, Grandier Ski Tours, Grandier Car Rentals, Grandier Hotel Construction, Grandier Travel Service.... The list continued. Pete whistled softly. Whatever he might have thought earlier, Grandier Limited was certainly for real.

An elevator reached the ground floor, delivering a dozen office workers, and Maggie and Pete slipped inside. Maggie pressed the button for the top floor and they rode up in silence, each of them puzzled now as to why Grandier Limited needed an interior decorator from America.

Moments later the doors opened on a spectacular

reception room. The bleached oak floor was covered with scattered nineteenth-century Kilum rugs; plants were separated among the gray-and-cream-colored sofas and chairs; and all was reflected in the polished steel of the high ceiling. The sudden beauty of the room momentarily stunned them, and they took it all in silently.

"May I help you?" The woman at the reception desk spoke sharply. She was not used to unexpected visitors; the top floor of the building was reserved for executive offices. This young couple, dressed for bad weather in boots, jeans, and leather jackets, were obviously strangers to Grandier.

"Is all this new?" Maggie asked, indicating the decorations.

"Yes, miss. Grandier Limited only recently moved into these quarters. May I help you?"

"Excuse me," Pete spoke up. "Is this the only Grandier building on Tottenham Court Road?"

"That's right. It's our only office in London. You are on the executive office level, but if you'll tell me what tourist services you require, I'll give you the floor number." She pulled out a note pad and looked up, waiting for them to reply.

Maggie glanced at Pete, and then said, smiling nicely at the woman, "I'm Maggie Walsh, from Los Angeles, California." She paused, waited a moment for the woman to recognize her name. When she didn't Maggie continued quickly. "I received a telegram on Monday afternoon from Mr. Grandier..." She paused again, then asked directly, "Would it be possible for me to see Mr. Grandier? I understand it is late in the day, but..."

"I am afraid it will not be possible," the woman replied.

"And why not?" Pete asked.

"Easy, Pete." Maggie touched his arm.

"Mr. Grandier is not in London, sir, nor do I expect him. Did you say you had an appointment?"

"Well, no," Maggie began, "but he sent me a telegram . . ." She fumbled for her wallet, regretting that she was wearing jeans. "Here it is!" She handed the telegram to the receptionist.

"This telegram didn't come from Grandier Limited," the woman stated, handing it back to Maggie.

"Well, perhaps someone besides Mr. Grandier . . ."

The receptionist kept shaking her head, disagreeing. "I see copies of all cables and letters that come out of this office. It is one of my responsibilities to file all cables, and I know this one was not sent from our offices."

"But this telegram commissions me to design and furnish Grandier's new office complex on Tottenham Court Road," Maggie said quickly, her voice rising.

"Well, as you can see we don't need our offices decorated. This is a new building and everyone is quite happy with the decor."

Pete asked, "Where might I locate Mr. Grandier? Is there somewhere I can telephone and leave a message telling him we're in London?"

"As I said, Mr. Grandier is rarely in London, sir. I don't actually expect him now for at least a month." She opened a schedule book on her desk.

"He's in Spain today, in the Sierra Nevada area. We're planning a new winter resort there." She flipped the pages of the book, and continued. "At the end of this week he's due in the Baleares, staying a few days at the Port Mahon Hotel in Minorca."

She closed the book and looked up, smiling, as if to show that not much happened at Grandier Limited without her knowledge. "If Mr. Grandier was planning on returning unexpectedly to London I would know." She paused, and added generously, "If you care to give me your names I'll mention them to Mr. Smyth—that's Mr. Grandier's personal assistant—when he telephones tomorrow. He'll be able to tell Mr. Grandier you stopped by."

"Thank you for your help," Pete said, when they gave the woman their names and were ready to leave.

"Not at all." She smiled back. "Are you staying in town this week? If so, I could ring you after I speak to Mr. Smyth."

"No, we'll call you. We're planning to tour Kent starting tomorrow." Pete motioned toward Maggie. "Her people come from somewhere in Kent. I guess we'll be spending the next few days searching graveyards for lost relatives."

They descended in silence to the marble lobby, and Maggie waited until they had pushed through the glass doors into the rain before she asked, "What do you think?"

"I think we should find a pub and get something to drink. I'm freezing."

"But do you make any sense of all that?"

"None whatsoever. Grandier Limited doesn't

need you or anyone else to decorate that office building."

"Then why the telegram?" Maggie was rushing to keep pace with his stride.

Pete shook his head. "Grandier is out of the country and no one has heard of you or Danner/Walsh Associates. It all looks phony except for one thing."

"What?" Maggie grabbed Pete's arm and stopped him. "What is it?"

"The money. No one is going to mail you a first-class ticket and ten thousand dollars without a reason. Grandier, whoever he is and wherever he is, has something in mind."

"Then what do we do?"

"On Monday morning we'll telephone. Until then"—he put his arm around Maggie and kissed her lightly—"we'll spend their money."

"And I don't have to worry about anything, Pete?" She was waiting for him to say everything was okay.

"You don't have to worry about a thing. On Monday this guy Smyth will clear it all up. And once you finish that job, everyone in England will know about Maggie Walsh."

"Even Grandier?" she said wryly.

"Grandier most of all," he said, and sealed his promise with a kiss.

Jacques Grandier sat on the open terrace of the Port Mahon Hotel, facing east toward the wide entrance of the harbor. He ordered a lunch of *cordonices con cerezas* and half a carafe of white wine, asking the captain to select a fine dry white for him.

In allowing the captain the opportunity to choose the wine, Jacques Grandier was giving the man a chance to display his knowledge and training. The captain did not know it, but his future career depended on what local wine he chose for this quiet middle-aged businessman. If he selected well, Grandier would take him from this small island in the shadow of Majorca and place him in one of Grandier Limited's luxury hotels on the Costa Blanca or the Costa del Azahar.

Most of the time, of course, he was poorly served by waiters in such places. But he never complained, nor drew attention to his importance; he liked to remain anonymous. Very little was actually known about Jacques Grandier and the mystery gave him a certain leverage in international circles.

George Smyth, his administrative assistant, sat across the table reading a letter from a building contractor in Monaco. While Smyth read aloud, Jacques ate his *ensalada naranja y queso*.

Sitting in the warm afternoon sun of the Mediterranean, he appeared prosperous and healthy, a large, well-built man with strong features, a dark, suntanned face, and short black hair fringed with gray. He was expensively dressed, wearing a Givenchy camel hair sports jacket, a silk shirt, light-tan Dior slacks, and handmade shoes by Beudetti of Florence. The only thing that revealed that Jacques Grandier was not born to wealth was the way he devoured his food. He was a man who ate only for nourishment, never for pleasure. It was the legacy of a childhood spent on the bleak coast of southern France during the Second World War, a time he remembered only as a nightmare.

His parents had been resistance fighters. When he was twelve years old, the Gestapo came to his family's farmhouse, in the countryside outside Marseilles. When Jacques returned from his chores, he found his mother in her kitchen, dead, machine-gunned. His father and older brothers he found later, in the fields. Their throats had been cut, and his father's chest pierced with his own pitchfork.

After that, Jacques Grandier lived for weeks without food. Then he joined up with a band of other homeless children, who survived only on the rodents they could run down in the fields and in the bombed-out village nearby. Even now, after all his years of success, he could not control himself before a plate of food. He would fall upon it hungrily, as if he were still that same starving child.

He had survived the terror of his youth, and promised himself he would never again return to such a helpless state. During the years he had developed Grandier Limited, he had dealt ruthlessly with anyone who tried to block him. The rumor was that he was not above killing to get his way. It was true; he had.

When Smyth finished reading, Jacques Grandier stopped eating long enough to give his reply:

"Cable our friend today," he said softly, almost apologetically. "Tell him I don't care what problems he's encountered. If he doesn't complete the hotel by September '81, the penalty is ten thousand pounds a week, and that figure will double automatically after three months. And remind him these were the conditions we agreed upon verbally last month, and if now he does not wish to honor his word, then he will never again put up as much as a beach umbrella on the Mediterranean." He picked up his fork and returned to the salad. "Now, George, find out what has happened to our wine."

"I think it is coming, sir." George saw the captain moving toward their table, but then noticed the man was carrying an extension telephone and not the wine.

Jacques Grandier looked up and saw the telephone. It did not surprise him. He demanded that his staff stay in touch by phone, but he let George handle the call while he stared out over the serene blue harbor. It was a lovely island, he thought. There *should* be a few unspoiled places left in the Mediterranean for himself and his friends.

"Mr. Grandier," George said quickly. "It's Ravenshurst."

Grandier nodded and hoped Smyth did not notice his sudden nervousness. It was always that way when Ravenshurst telephoned. He wondered if the others also tensed up when a call came from Jason.

His assistant handed Grandier the receiver. Without being told, Smyth stood and left the table, leaving Grandier alone on the sunny terrace.

When Smyth was out of hearing, Grandier said in English into the receiver, "Yes, Jason?"

But it was not Jason telephoning.

"Mr. Grandier," Adams said, "Mr. Mountolive has asked me to contact you."

"Yes, Adams, what is it?"

"Mr. Mountolive wishes you to be at Ravens-hurst this weekend."

"This weekend? . . . I'm afraid that might be a bit difficult. I'm in the Balearics today and I must fly to the Costa del Azahar tomorrow. May I speak with Jason a moment?"

"I'm sorry, that is not possible," Adams replied curtly. "I have been instructed to tell you that Mr. Mountolive has located number six."

The news shocked Jacques. It was a moment before he could respond. "That's wonderful, Adams." He knew his voice lacked enthusiasm.

"We will expect you then tomorrow," Adams stated.

"Yes, of course." Grandier rushed to agree, but he could not concentrate. The sixth had been found. The circle was completed.

"Who is it, Adams?"

"It is a young woman, Mr. Grandier. A young woman from America."

When he hung up, Grandier's hands were still trembling. Smyth was coming back across the terrace, bringing the waiter with their lunch, but Jacques no longer had the time for quail.

"George, we have a change of plans." He smiled, trying to appear buoyant. "Call the airport and have the plane prepared. Tell them I want to fly directly to Gatwick."

"Yes, sir." George Smyth accepted these new instructions without question. Their plans always changed when a call came from Ravenshurst. "Is that all, sir?"

"Yes, thank you, George." Grandier's voice was steady, unemotional. But Smyth's eyes went to Grandier's lap, where his hands were trembling, his fingers convulsively twisting his strange, silver signet ring.

Chapter Three

EARLY THE NEXT MORNING, they rented the Triumph
Bonneville near Edgeware Road. They left their
luggage with the porter and by ten o'clock had
packed the bike's saddlebags with what they
thought they might need for a few days on the road.
Then they crossed the River Thames at London
Bridge, found the road to Rochester and headed
southeast for Kent.

It was Pete's plan not to stop until they reached
"quaint" old England, the England of village pubs
and thatched cottages. But in Rochester, a city as
crowded and busy as any in America, he stopped to
show Maggie the Charles Dickens museum, then

drove slowly down High Street, pointing out all the ancient store fronts and the second-hand furniture stores. He was a perfect guide; like Maggie, Pete loved old buildings and antique furnishings, and the stories of people and events that made all the places famous.

They left Rochester for Maidstone, stopping on the way to eat a lunch of fruit and cheese on the banks of the Medway River near Allington Castle. It was after two o'clock and the afternoon was warm enough for Maggie to lie back on the grass and relax in the sun while Pete finished eating and explained the sightseeing trip he had planned.

"We'll head toward Canterbury next, Mag," he said, studying the map of Kent, "but we're not going to be in a hurry. I want to get off these main arteries and pick up what the English call 'unclassified' roads."

"Could we stay at an inn tonight?" she asked. "A country inn with a fireplace in the bedroom and a canopy bed?" It made her feel good just thinking of being in bed with him, snug and warm under heavy quilts.

"Sure we can. We can do anything you want. We have no schedule, no plans, no worries. We'll just follow these back roads and country lanes to wherever they go, okay?"

From Allington Castle, they followed the Medway River, through the town of Maidstone east toward Hollingbourne.

"This is the prettiest village in England," Pete said over his shoulder as he maneuvered the bike up the main street, past all the Tudor houses and cottages. At Colepeper Hall, at the top of the hill, he stopped the bike.

"The Colepepers were an important family at the time of Henry the Eighth," he said. "Katherine Howard, Henry the Eighth's fifth wife, once had an affair with a Colepeper. You're not a Colepeper or a Howard, are you?"

"Stop it!" Maggie protested, laughing at his attempt to give her a scandalous family background. "My family got along with Henry the Eighth; it was his daughter, Elizabeth, who gave them trouble." She linked her arm to his and they started to walk through the small village, climbing the hill into the woods above.

"But your mother's name is Walsingham. Francis Walsingham was Queen Elizabeth's Secretary of State, and one of her most distinguished statesmen. Elizabeth didn't like him much, but he was a loyal servant to the Crown. Elizabeth wouldn't kick his family out of England."

"Maybe my family came from another Walsingham. Is that possible?"

"Oh, sure, it's a famous English name. Must have been dozens of them. Edmund Walsingham was the jailor at the Tower of London."

"What about women, weren't there any Walsingham women?"

"I guess, but women seldom made it into history books unless they married kings."

Remounting the bike, they rode to the crest of the hill, six hundred feet above sea level, and could see across to the Isle of Oxney. The land stretched below them in a patchwork pattern of green meadows fenced by rock walls and small streams. The fields were empty except for flocks of sheep that moved over the lowlands like endless summer clouds.

Pete stopped the bike again and they stood for a moment, watching.

"This is really England, Mag," he said. "This is the real old County Kent, the home of Chaucer, Dickens, and Henry the Eighth's second wife, not to mention Maggie Walsh."

"Show-off!" She laughed. "I can't remember which wife was the second—Anne of Cleves?"

"You're close—Anne Boleyn. She married Henry and got her head cut off for her trouble. But don't worry, you're not royalty." Pete started the bike, and pushed off.

"But I am! I am," she protested, her words lost as the bike picked up speed. "I just know I am."

Barbara Kirstenburg stood before the floor-to-ceiling mirror in her office and let the reporter wait. Always let them wait and always make them pay— those were the business principles Jason had taught her, and she had been a willing student. She smiled, remembering. But Jason had always been a charmer, a flirt, if one could use that word to describe Jason. He had never made the slightest suggestion or overture to her—and, oh, how she had wished he would ask. But he had only smiled with those wonderfully blue eyes and kissed her hand, as if it were still before the war and she were a Russian princess. Maybe he had thought she was too old for him.

She did not look forty-five, this she knew positively. She could tell by the looks men gave her, out on the Avenue Montaigne. All the most important *maisons de la couture*, including her own, were here on the Right Bank. The most beautiful women in the world walked these streets, but Barbara was not intimidated by them. She was a beautiful and talented person. Jason had given her that confidence.

The young American reporter was still waiting. Barbara knew she had to see her, even though she was hectically busy in her *atélier*, her workshop, preparing for the fall collection.

She turned from the mirror and looked around her office. It occupied the top floor of the town house that was also the headquarters of her company. Unlike the other elegant rooms of the maison, her office was crowded with bolts of fabric and discarded sketches. She liked the disorder—it suggested action and power—but she had softened the effect by having the walls painted a lovely *feuille morte*, her favorite yellow-brown shade.

She stepped to the desk and buzzed Etienne, her secretary, telling him to admit the reporter from America.

"Miss Kirstenburg, who was important to you in developing your fashion style?" Taffy Scott asked. They had discussed the fall collection for an hour, and now the reporter was summing up.

"Well, certainly Lucien Lelong. Dior once quoted Lucien as saying that each fabric has a personality, and is as unpredictable as a woman.

That is why I believe that haute couture must begin with the fabric, not the design. The fabric must first speak to me, tell me what to do with it."

"It's been said of St. Laurent," the reporter commented, "that he manages to blend the worlds of Chekhov, Colette, and even the North African Berbers. Does that seem true to you?"

"Oh yes. People tend to forget that Yves was born in North Africa, after all. Have you ever been to his home in Marrakech? Lovely."

Taffy Scott shook her head and went on. "Could we take a moment to trace the influences in *your* work? You were born in southern France, I know, but your family is Russian, correct?"

"Yes, that's so," Barbara began. She was asked this question often, and she glanced at herself in the large mirror as she rattled off her pat answer. "My parents escaped Russia shortly before the revolution and managed to bring out most of their fortune. A few of the jewels had to be left behind, of course, but I was fortunate enough to grow up in a wonderful atmosphere of luxury and good taste. My mother and her friends were dressed by Chanel, and Coco often visited our house in Nice."

"That small chest over in the corner," said the reporter, "the *semainier*—I noticed it once in the Chanel *atélier*. Did you buy it from her estate?"

Barbara paused, her eyes narrowing. The woman was not a typical American fashion reporter. "No, mademoiselle," she said coldly. "It was a gift from Coco, bequeathed to me in her will. Now, is that all? They await me downstairs, in the *atélier*."

The reporter continued to smile. "Just a few more facts to check, madame, if you don't mind. As you must be aware, Miss Kirstenburg, along the Right Bank it is rumored that your family were not wealthy White Russians. They say you rose to riches in the fashion world with the help of an influential English gentleman, a man of mystery who is your financier, as well as your particularly close friend." The reporter kept her eyes on the famous couturier, watching for a sign of alarm.

Barbara Kirstenburg only smiled, sweetly, disarmingly. She seemed amused. "Oh, are they still spreading those silly rumors? We are all plagued by them—Marc, Oscar, Hubert, all of us. Yves is the only one who takes gossip to heart, though. He is so sensitive."

"This cannot be classified as gossip," the reporter protested. "The research I've done proves that you were born, not of White Russians, but of a poor family in Riga, Latvia. Furthermore, the Englishman I mentioned was linked to you in 1959, when Pauline Conte was stabbed. There is a photograph of you leaving the courthouse with Mr.—"

"Stop! Stop it!" Barbara screamed, then turned to her secretary, who had rushed in at the sound of her cry. "Etienne, get this woman out of my office, out of my maison."

The reporter slowly gathered her purse and coat. "This will not stop my investigation, Miss Kirstenburg," she said.

"Yes, it will, Miss Scott," said Barbara evenly, in control again. "Your access to the great houses of Paris is over. You are banned from the showings, from the *prêt-à-porter* collections at the Porte de Versailles, even from the showrooms on Seventh Avenue. Your editor will be notified by her superiors that you are an embarrassment to the *Times*, and you will be reassigned, perhaps to Iran. A very dangerous place, as I understand it, Miss Scott.

"Do not doubt my power to carry out these threats. As you should know, my connections are very powerful. You sought to embarrass me, mademoiselle; instead you have ruined yourself. Etienne! *S'il vous plaît . . .*"

As the young reporter left, trembling, Barbara sat down at her gilt desk. She would speak to Jason about the girl immediately; by that evening New York would have received instructions.

But before she could direct Etienne to place the call, her lucite telephone began to ring. It was Ravenshurst calling, Adams telephoning to tell her to come immediately. Jason wanted her.

Chapter Four

THE INN THEY FOUND was in the middle of town, on the busy High Street. There was a noisy pub on the main floor and a larger restaurant behind, but the woman told Pete the room was quiet and he said okay.

"I call it my honeymoon suite," the woman said, leading them upstairs and down the hall to the back of the inn. "Of course," she added, smiling kindly at Maggie, "it isn't a suite at all, just this one room, but we think it's lovely. Especially now in winter. It gets the afternoon light, you see."

The room was tiny and clean and made up like a child's doll house.

"Oh, it's lovely," Maggie whispered, her face

sparkling. The afternoon sun splashed across the old-fashioned wallpaper like paint, and spotlighted the canopy bed, done up in rich pink brocade. There was only the bed, an easy chair by the fireplace, and a few pieces of Georgian furniture.

"Yes, it is lovely, isn't it?" The woman gazed fondly around, setting the key on the dresser.

"Dinner is at eight sharp, but the pub is open, if you'd like to pop in for a minute. If you need anything just ring. I'll have Charlie come up and set the fire."

"Thank you," Maggie answered, and moved toward the door, as if to herd the woman from the room.

"You might want to open the windows," the woman added, standing in the doorway and trying to look past Maggie. "It gets quite warm when the fire is lit."

"Thank you," Maggie said again, slowly closing the door. The woman was still in the hall, still smiling, her cheeks blazing like roses.

"I think she wanted to stay and watch," Pete said.

"Shhh!" Maggie giggled. "She'll hear you."

Pete tossed the saddlebags on the chair. "What a weirdo. Sure she's not a relative?"

"Oh, stop! Obviously she knows we're lovers and it just makes her happy to see us. Maybe she thinks it's our honeymoon!"

"Won't she be surprised, then, when the first thing we do is go downstairs to grab a pint? Ready?"

"Oh, you go ahead if you want. I need a bath. I'll meet you downstairs later, okay?"

The bath, he knew, was mostly an excuse. She

wanted to be alone, and he didn't blame her. They both needed space.

"I'll tip a few with the locals," he said, "and you can take over the tub. You don't have to come downstairs. I'll meet you back here." He kissed her on the bridge of her nose and swung off the bed.

The room was darkening, but Maggie could see well enough to undress and sort out her clothes. First she hung her jeans and the heavy white sweater on the back of the chair. These she'd have to wear again the next day, for they had only packed one change of clothes in the saddlebags.

Then she went in to run water for her tub. It was an old-fashioned bathroom with exposed steam pipes, and a tub that stood off the floor, supported by feet shaped like lion's paws.

She had packed a bottle of Benandré bath oil and she poured it into the steaming water before pinning up her hair and sliding slowly into the tub. Tucking a towel behind her neck she stretched her legs, sighing at the relief of having them straight. All day she had ridden on the back of the bike, her legs held up tight against Pete. Now she could float freely in the hot water as the steam rose and clouded the mirror with mist, making the small room steam like a sauna.

"Signorina?" The maid stood near the tub holding a large egg-white bath towel in both hands and waited for Maria Gabrielli to acknowledge her. The signorina lay on her back in the huge, sunken tub, her body deep in hot water slick with bath oil. On a floating tray, she had propped up a copy of

Paris-Match which she read while eating slices of a peeled orange.

"Signorina!" The maid tried again. She knew how her mistress hated to leave the warm bathtub. "Signorino Sciolino is waiting. He has been already one hour..."

"Tell Signorino Sciolino to go screw himself," Maria snapped back and rolled over in the deep tub, splashing water onto the pink tile floor.

"Oh, Signorina!" The maid blessed herself.

"Don't carry on, Tattie," Maria interrupted. "If you keep this up, you can go keep house for the Curia. Now, where is Signorino Sciolino?"

"In your sitting room."

"Send him in." She removed the magazine and the floating tray and slipped further into the deep pool of water. There were blue and green lights deep inside and they played softly against her nude body.

Signorino Renato Sciolino came quietly into the bedroom. He had never been to the top floor, the inner sanctum of the house on Via Ludovisi, though he knew that sometimes Maria invited special friends to her apartment. His father had told him as much.

"Renato?" she called out. "I'm in here, darling." She had a soft, smooth voice. In the years since leaving Naples, she had eradicated the harsh sounds of her childhood Italian, learned on the streets near the Piazza del Mercato. It was only when she was angry that she reverted to her slum dialect and exposed her upbringing.

Renato Sciolino moved slowly through the white bedroom toward the lighted doorway of the bathroom. He stepped cautiously forward and looked in. Maria smiled up at him from the pool. He was younger than she, not yet twenty-five, and had the clean looks of a student. But he had dressed well for this encounter, wearing his new suit from Adolfo Dominguez. And he had brought her flowers.

"Oh, Renato, how sweet." She smiled. Flowers pleased her, but they also made her sad, for they died so quickly, even in water. "Here!" she demanded, reaching for them. She rose up in the water and her breasts, pink and wet from the heat, emerged. The sudden sight of them, the warm intimacy of the bathroom, made the boy blush and hesitate.

"Oh, Renato," she scolded, "don't be bashful. You are making me feel like your mama. You have seen a woman before, no?" She kept smiling, mocking him. "Is it too warm maybe, my little one? Come here, bambino."

He was such a pretty boy. Too pretty, she thought, with his long curly black hair, slight body, and the eyes of a cat. He was not at all like his father, heir to none of his father's charm and graciousness. Yet she had to be nice to him. It was his father's wish and that wish was not to be taken lightly.

Renato knelt down near the pool, enthralled by her body, and she reached to loosen his tie only to splash bathwater down the leg of his suit trousers. "Oh, Renato," she giggled, "you have gone peepee!" She fell into the pool, splashing another wave of water onto the tile floor.

He scurried back, trying to escape the water. It was the first time he had worn the suit and he had been afraid even to sit down and ruin the perfectly pressed crease.

"Goddamn you!" He threw the red roses at her and she screamed and then laughed as the roses filled the pool, the tender petals floating in the warm water.

"Oh, Renato," she said, "you have spoiled these lovely roses."

"I don't give a goddamn about those flowers." He was standing in the doorway, his feet apart and his fists clenched.

She began to pick the petals from the pool, then stopped. They were in a way much lovelier this way, scattered and dismembered. She glanced up at Renato. He was still panting and angry, but his small eyes had lost their meanness and he did not know what to do. Now she had to say something sweet, something to let him maintain his sense of macho.

"Renato, please." She touched the edge of the pool. "I'm sorry for misbehaving."

"Do you ever leave this tub?" he asked, smiling.

Maria sighed. It would not be so bad; he was trying to be nice. Perhaps his father had given him instructions as well. She shook her head no.

"Never?" He found a dry edge of the tile and sat down. He had long legs and his knees stuck up in the air awkwardly. "Then how do you make love?" he asked, gaining more confidence. This woman, he saw, was afraid of him, of who he was and what he could do to her.

"Well, I make love here," she said. "It is quite nice, no? Have you made love in a pool?" She was being coquettish but it bored her. "Come, Renato, get rid of all those lovely clothes." She slid over in the wide bath, as if to make room for him.

He undressed in her bedroom, taking care to lay out his clothes so they would not wrinkle. He even folded his underwear and he took his time. He wanted her to wait. When he was ready, he returned and stood before her.

His body did not excite her. He was too tall and thin, all legs and arms, like a colt. But she had her job to do, even if it was boring.

"Come," she beckoned, enticing him toward the deep warm pool of water, but he was still reluctant. He was frightened, she could see, uncertain of how to perform in this strange setting, but she would subdue his arrogance.

Renato was kissing her face. Sitting on the edge of the pool with his feet dangling in the water, he was smothering her with sloppy kisses. He had the enthusiasm, she thought, of a lap dog, and the sex appeal. But she endured it. She had trained herself to divorce this physical act from her conscience, to make love and not be violated.

It was Jason who had taught her, back in Naples, that one must give away only the nonessential parts of one's life. Her body was not important, he told her. It was negotiable. But her spirit mattered and had to be protected.

She could still see him, looking so handsome and distinguished on that dingy side street, and speaking flawless Italian in his crisp British accent. "Save your soul for what really matters in this world," he had said, and then given her the ring, slipping it easily onto her finger. How long ago had that been? She had been just fifteen when he found her on the streets near Porta Capuano. Now she was thirty.

"Take it off," Renato ordered.

"What, my sweet?" She noticed with satisfaction that at least he had slipped into the water.

"That chain and cross." He waved impatiently at her gold necklace.

"Ah, you are still afraid of the nuns' stories." She mocked him again, laughing at his religious superstition. "You won't touch a woman who wears a cross?"

He slapped her once hard across the face and it spun her head and stung. She had to grab hold of the tub's edge to keep from slipping under.

When she pulled herself up, her tolerance toward him was over. "Renato," she said quietly, containing her anger, "you are very young. I forgive you for what you have done, because of your age, and because of your father. I do not wish to hurt Giovanni Sciolino's son, but I must warn you that men even more influential than Giovanni have hurt my girls and suffered because of it. You are too young and stupid to understand who I am and what power I have in the city of Rome. I will let this insult pass, but now you must leave."

He hit her again, a blow that snapped her head back and bloodied her nose. She fell against the tile tub and slipped into the water.

"You bitch! You don't tell me when to leave." He picked her up, lifting her from the water. She had swallowed a mouthful and gasped while she fought against him, cursing and swinging wildly. If she could get free for a moment, she could ring the buzzer for help. Paolo and Ugo were both working at the bar. She tried to swing again, but was too tired. Staying so long in the water had exhausted her.

She screamed instead. Her high-pitched voice echoed in the big, tile bathroom and he hit her a third time, cutting her lip, and now she was frightened. His eyes had again that gray meanness. He would hurt her, she realized. The boy was crazy. He might even kill her.

Turning, she pulled away from him, back into the water, but he jumped in after, cursing and swinging at her. She reached to the other side and pressed the buzzer, holding the button down so they would know she needed help.

Renato grabbed Maria again and yanked her up. Her body was wet and slippery from sweat and water and she could not resist him. He was too strong, too big for her. He was trying to force himself into her when the bartenders reached the bathroom and grabbed him, pulling him onto his back and stuffing his head in the water. Ugo took hold of Renato's hair with one hand and held a knife under the boy's chin. Paolo jumped into the pool and drove his knee into Renato's chest, knocking the air from his lungs and pinning him against the bottom.

"Don't kill him," Maria said evenly. She had stepped from the water and wrapped her robe tightly around her. "Get him dressed," she said as she walked into the bedroom, "and bring him to me."

She had combed out her hair and was putting on makeup when they brought Renato before her, holding him between them like a wet dog. He had regained his insolent attitude and said quickly, challenging her:

"You don't dare hurt me. If you do, my father

will close your house down."

Ugo hit the boy again in the stomach and Renato doubled over, his legs buckling under him.

"Wait, Ugo," Maria said patiently, and let Renato recover before saying: "You are a foolish boy, but you are not a child and therefore you are responsible for your actions. I will talk to your father myself and tell him of your behavior. He can do what he wishes, but for myself, I am telling you never to return to my house."

"Do you think my father will believe you, a whore, and not his own son?"

Maria did not answer. Instead she spoke to her two employees. "Take him out by the back door and dump him in the alley. Do not kill him, but make sure he will always remember who I am."

She returned to the mirror and continued to make up her face, forcing the vulgar incident from her mind. The telephone rang before she finished, a call on her private line, and she picked it up, knowing who was calling. He always knew when she was troubled. It was Ravenshurst, and Adams was on the line telling her to come to Kent immediately.

Chapter Five

MAGGIE STIRRED IN THE TUB. She had fallen asleep and when she woke the water had cooled. It was late, and Pete would be back and wanting to take a bath himself. She heard footsteps in the room and called, "Pete, it's all yours." Then she stepped from the tub and wrapped her long hair in a blue towel before she began to dry herself.

The room was chilly after the warmth of the bathwater, and she shivered. Pete had packed his white terry-cloth robe, she remembered.

"Hey, in there," she called through the half-open door, "would you bring me your robe? I'm freezing." She could hear him moving around the room, but he didn't answer. Impatiently she walked into the bedroom. "The robe, huh, Pete?" she demanded.

The bedroom was almost dark, lit only by the bright, warm fire. She could see his shadow at the window.

"Oh, a fire! It's wonderful." She moved immediately to warm herself and saw then that the dark figure by the window was not Pete. The man was too broad and muscular. She could not see his face, but he was standing still, watching her naked body. She could not move or speak; her fear had frozen the breath in her throat.

The man said something but she didn't understand, and then he moved forward.

"Don't, please. I have money. You can have my money."

He kept coming, stepping into the ring of firelight. He was tall and stoop-shouldered with a pockmarked face and small eyes, shadowed by a brown cap. He wore old farm clothes, a dirty leather vest, and big black overshoes. In his right hand he carried a wooden log the length of a club.

"It's me, miss." He grinned, showing a mouthful of decaying teeth.

"Please, don't!" Her fear finally made her move. She could feel the cold stone of the hearth as she backed toward the flame. The fire singed her legs as he forced her backward. This is impossible, she told herself. It couldn't be happening to her. They were on vacation in England. Where was Pete?

"It's me, ma'am. Charlie."

"Charlie—?"

The door opened and Pete stepped in, stopping abruptly at the entrance. He saw Maggie naked in front of the fire, confronting the inn's handyman who had been sent up to start the fire.

"Pete!" Her fear broke when she saw him and she ran to him.

"What the hell is going on?" Pete pulled her into his arms. The handyman dropped the piece of wood Maggie had taken for a club and ran out, his heavy boots thumping on the hallway floors.

"Oh, God, Pete. He was going to attack me. I thought it was you and I came out of the bathroom... I couldn't see... He was so horrible-looking..." Her tears choked her and she broke down into convulsive tears.

Firmly Pete sat her on the bed and wrapped a quilt around her.

"Maggie, honey, he wasn't going to hurt you." He couldn't keep from smiling. He knew she was still terrified, but it had been only a silly mistake. "He works here at the inn. Remember, the old lady said Charlie would come up and make a fire? I saw him down at the pub and told him it was okay to go up. I'm sorry. I didn't realize you'd get frightened."

"Oh, Christ." She sighed. "I don't believe..." and then she burst into laughter and fell back on the bed. "I thought he was going to kill me. I thought he was going to bludgeon me to death with that stick of wood."

"Not in England, Maggie. Nothing is going to happen to you."

She pulled him down beside her, immensely relieved but exhausted from her siege of fear.

"Don't leave me alone again, okay? I don't feel safe in these foreign countries. And don't tell me I'm not a foreigner. I have no more feeling for England

or Kent than anyone else. I'm an American, thank
God, and England depresses me. I can't explain it,
but I feel strange and nervous all the time."

"Nothing is going to go wrong, Maggie." He
pulled her into the safety of his arms. "Nothing is
going to happen to you."

The old German stood at his open window high
up in the Addis Ababa Hilton and looked out over
the sprawling capital city of Ethiopia, watching the
violent sun descend across the Rift Valley. He took
a cigarette from a gold Cartier case and lit it while he
watched the African city.

It was a beautiful evening. The winter rains had
left the city washed, and the wine-red sun sparkled
off the tin roofs of the acres of hovels that crowded
the hillside below Mount Entoto. From the
window, the city looked like a scrap heap scattered
on the lush green landscape.

The old man watched until the city disappeared
into darkness and only ribbons of street lights
etched the borders of the wide, deserted boulevards.
Then the shooting began, distant and sporadic at
first—an occasional rifle shot, a burst of machine-
gun fire—and finally the fierce, urgent sirens of the
military police cars. It was always that way in
Ethiopia. At night the killings began.

He closed the window and pulled the heavy
curtains. He moved slowly, for at night, especially in
the damp weather, his leg stiffened. His fatigue
annoyed him. He had arrived earlier that week from
Germany and the thin air of the mountain country
had quickly tired him. He was too old to be flying
out to Africa. It was a job for younger men. But

when there was a problem, he was the only one who could deal with it. He could figure the costs, decide if the risks were worthwhile, and judge whether the profits were high enough to kill for. Usually they were.

The fact that he was willing to kill, he realized, made him superior to other men. It had made him successful in life. He was sure it was what had attracted Jason's attention. Jason had said as much the first time he came to the German's aid, keeping him out of prison that time in Malaysia.

He poured himself a whiskey from a flask he had brought—he trusted neither the food, the water, nor the liquor in any African country—and prepared himself to wait. Eventually his men would find the Ethiopian and bring him to the Hilton; it was just a matter of time.

Over the years he had come to learn that waiting was a talent as valuable as any. What was essential was knowing when to wait and when to strike. Jason had taught him that lesson. Jason had taught him more than he had taught the others but, then, Karl Liebknecht had known Jason longer than any of them.

He sipped the whiskey and watched his reflection in the mirror. There was very little light in the room—he wanted the bedroom dark when Seifu arrived—but still he could see himself, shadowy in the glass. His face in the mirror always surprised him. People said he had aged well, but he hated the physical frailties that the years brought. His thick blond hair had thinned and turned white. His body had failed him, wasted away. Even so, he was still stronger, at seventy-five, than most men half his age. But his tall, rangy body had had to be resilient. It had survived much in Germany—two world wars, imprisonment, and those years of poverty in West Berlin.

But his own strength would not have been enough. Thank God he'd had Jason. Jason his good friend. The old man wiped sentimental tears from his eyes and straightened up in the chair. Why had Jason not aged? He always remained the same: the proper English gentleman, healthy, strong, and energetic. Once he had asked Jason how he kept his youthful looks, and Jason had only smiled and shaken his head. It was another secret of Jason Mountolive.

Then the door burst open and the waiting was over. His two men appeared, holding the struggling Ethiopian between them as if he were their prisoner instead of their partner.

The young man was small and slight, dressed poorly in a patchwork of discarded western clothes. He looked frantically around the dark room, the whites of his eyes flashing as the two Germans pinned him into a wooden straight-back chair, tying his arms quickly behind him, and then strapping his legs to the wooden frame.

The old man waited until his people had secured the Ethiopian and still he did not hurry. He had all night, and the Ethiopian did not have much to tell him. One of his men turned on a light, tilting the shade so the African was caught in the glare. The young man looked around wildly. He knew Karl Liebknecht had to be somewhere in the room, but the bright light blinded him and he could see nothing.

Now Karl stood and moved closer. His leg was stiffer and pain stabbed him in the thigh. He had to grab the end of the bed to keep from falling, but neither of his men rushed to help. They knew the penalty for appearing to notice his one physical weakness. Outside the frame of light he stopped, still concealed by the darkness, and spoke to the young Ethiopian in English, his perfect sentence construction ruined only by a heavy accent.

"Ato Seifu, we have had a misunderstanding." It was always his way to be polite, to give them the benefit of the doubt, all the while knowing the outcome of the interrogation.

The Ethiopian began to shake his head, to explain and deny in broken English, but the old man stepped forward with surprising agility and hit the young man across his dark cheek. The Ethiopian's head popped back from the fierce blow. Even the two German aides flinched, taken by surprise. Usually Der Führer, as they sometimes called him, liked to play cat and mouse a little longer.

"No excuses, Seifu!" Karl leaned forward so his face came into the light. "We made an agreement in Berlin. You wanted weapons—mine detectors, howitzers, tanks, anti-aircraft missiles." He was whispering, not shouting, but the words stung the Ethiopian. "All you revolutionaries are the same. Modern weapons are your salvation. But where is the money for your ideological revolutions?"

The Ethiopian tried to speak, but Liebknecht hit him again, this time breaking open a lip. Then he continued, "I have taken chances for your people, broken the German law against exporting arms. I have shipped the weapons unassembled into Italy, then down the Red Sea to the Sudan. And where is my money? You told me it would be placed in Swiss banks."

"It was, sir." Seifu answered without lifting his head. Blood from his lip stained his European shirt and now the lip was swelling up so he could hardly speak.

Karl stood and straightened himself, touched his tie back into place, and combed back his thin white hair with a brush of his hand. He sighed and stepped out of the circle of light, dragging his bad leg as he moved.

"A few hundred thousand Swiss francs is nothing, Seifu," he explained, as if teaching a lesson to a student.

"The rest is coming, sir." Seifu looked up, sensing that he had passed the danger point. "The Arabs have promised—"

Liebknecht snorted. "Do not quote me the Arabs. More revolutionary fools. You saw how heroic they were in Eritrea. The Cubans ran your countrymen into the sea and the Arabs did nothing." Karl sighed. Dealing with these people wearied and degraded him. The Krupps had it much easier; they never had to deal with these Africans who deserved no weapon more sophisticated than a spear. "I am not interested in your politics, Seifu, or your so-called Marxist struggle. Your weapons are in the Sudan and I want my money. The money we agreed on in Berlin last May."

"I swear on my mother's grave . . ."

The telephone rang on the desk, a quick, sudden barrage of urgent rings. It made them all start except Karl, who silently motioned one of his men to pick up the receiver.

There was no reason for the desk to ring his room. No one knew he was in Ethiopia. Except the local CID, of course. His face had no doubt been spotted at the airport; West Germany's leading weapons dealer could not enter Ethiopia unnoticed. Perhaps Seifu's guerrillas had followed him to the hotel. But that was of no concern. He knew that he and his two men could handle any number of Africans, Arabs or Jews.

But it was not a threatening call. It came long-distance from England and he hurried to take the receiver. He had not considered the possibility of Ravenshurst calling. Of course they would know where he was. They always knew.

"Mr. Liebknecht, is that you?"

"Yes, Adams, what is it?" Karl turned away from his men so they could not see the reaction on his face.

"Mr. Mountolive needs you."

"There's nothing wrong, is there, Adams?"

"She has been found, sir. Number six. You must be in England."

"I understand," he whispered, and thought: finally it is over. "Thank you, Adams. I will return immediately."

He stood for a moment, the receiver shaking in his trembling hand as he comprehended what Adams had told him. Slowly he hung up the phone. The others were waiting, watching him. One of his aides spoke up in German, asking what he wanted them to do with Seifu.

Karl glanced at the frightened Ethiopian, still shackled to the chair. Punishing him no longer mattered; even the money no longer mattered. Everything was rendered insignificant by the telephone call.

"I don't care," he said absently, dismissing the problem. "Kill him. Feed him to the crocodiles in the Nile. I am returning immediately to Europe, to Ravenshurst."

Chapter Six

"Do you want to make love or eat dinner?" Pete asked. They lay on the bed, their arms wrapped about each other.

"Let's have dinner. I'm starving," she said. "Okay?"

"Sure." He smiled, but he was disappointed. They hadn't made love since leaving California, and he could tell she was putting it off, delaying another encounter. He had done his best: a charming inn with a canopy bed and a warm fireplace. It was up to her.

"I do want to make love, Pete," she said, reading his thoughts. "And when I have a chance to relax, maybe drink some wine and get warm, I'll feel

better. But now, you know, after my visit from
Charlie the handyman, I just don't feel right."

"It's okay; I'm not pushing." He pulled himself
loose and swung off the bed, his feet hitting the
wooden floor hard as he bounced to his feet. "Are
we going to dress for dinner, madam?"

"Dress? All I have with me is jeans and those gray
trousers. I mean, do we have to dress?"

"No, hardly. You should see the locals in the pub.
They're right out of the fields. You look fine. You
always look fine, Maggie Walsh." He took her back
into his arms, and she hugged him.

"Why are you so nice to me?" she asked, half
joking.

"Because I love you."

That silenced her. It gave her goose pimples when
he told her that. She knew he loved her. It was
obvious in the way he stared at her, that helpless,
totally committed look. It frightened her, the
responsibility of his love. What would he do if they
didn't stay together? Falling in love with her had
ruined him in a curious way. He loved her regardless
of how she hurt him or what she asked of him.

She kissed him lightly on the lips and said,
"Dinner downstairs, dessert up here."

"You think you're just terrific, don't you?"

"Yes, and so do you." She kissed him once more,
then broke away. "Come on," she said, "let's check
out the food. Look at it this way: England can't get
any worse."

There was sunlight. Blazing, bright and blinding.
Every time he attempted to open his eyes, the light
burned them. He moved to escape the sunlight and

his head hurt. A steady jab of pain kept striking the base of his skull.

"Oh, my lord." He rolled to one side and finally escaped the late afternoon sun. Now he could feel cool sea wind. He opened his eyes carefully and discovered he was on the floor, his cheek flush against a deep matted carpet, his body wedged between an upholstered chair and the end of the bed.

It was a hotel room. He spotted his one piece of Gucci luggage in the corner. It was open and his clothes spilled over the sides. What was he doing in a hotel room? And where was he?

A wave of sea wind. It blew through the open French doors and cooled his face like a damp towel. He could see the room's terrace and a sky the color of the gulf stream. His location still eluded him, but he wasn't concerned. He had awakened before in such a drunken state, his mind blank and unfocused. The answer would come to him in time.

He sat at the foot of the bed, his head resting against the mattress, and looked toward the French doors. Key West. Yes, he remembered. He had flown down from Miami the day before in Billy's plane. And then they had started drinking at the Chart Room, moving on to Sloppy Joe's and Capt' Tony's, up and down Duval Street, through old Key West. He was at the Pier House Hotel, looking toward the Gulf of Mexico. And his name was Clive Jackson.

Well, he couldn't be too drunk. He could still remember his name.

The bed moved. Someone was getting up. Clive turned his head carefully to the right and avoided the piercing pain. Several inches from his eyes, a girl's leg hung over the end of the bed.

"Clive?"

A girl's voice.

"Here, luv." He had no idea who she was.

The girl bounced off the bed, walked naked across the room and stepped out onto the terrace, stretching herself in the warm day. Her back was to him and he did remember the body. All he could tell was that she was tiny, with long blond hair that touched her waist, and that she was very young.

"Hello," he said, trying to be friendly.

She spun around on her toes and smiled. "Oh, Clive," she answered, "it's terrific!"

She had blue eyes, the face of a fourteen-year-old, and she knew his name. He was in trouble. He made it to the edge of the bed and sat precariously, supporting his head in his hands.

"Are you going to be okay, Clive?" the little girl asked, as if she were talking to her father. He was only twenty-four, for God's sake. Although even that probably seemed old to a fourteen-year-old.

"Do you have a name, luv?" he managed to ask.

"Muffy. Did you forget it already?" She was hurt, sitting naked beside him. She was brown all over, not even a thin line of white inside her thigh. She looked like something one might find on a tropical beach, all brown and blond. "Last night you said it was terrific. You said you had never met anyone named Muffy."

"'Tis true, luv." He straightened up to deal with this.

"God, you look awful!"

He could see genuine disgust in her adolescent face. He was beginning to despise the little bitch.

"Where's Billy?" he asked. Suddenly he felt very ill and he had to swallow quick to keep from vomiting.

"Billy, your friend?"

"That's right, the crazy Yank."

"He's with Sherri."

"Sherri?"

"Sherri, my girl friend. Don't you remember? She has hair like mine, but not as long. People think we're twins, but we're not even sisters. She's my best friend from school."

"School? And where's that, Muffy?" He was having difficulty making conversation, staying awake, but he had to, now. If he passed out, she'd be off with his money. Six years ago, when he had first started promoting rock groups, he had learned not to trust any groupie, especially the blond, squeaky-clean types like her. They had the fast fingers.

"I don't want to talk about it." She stared off into the room.

"Well, where are Sherri and Billy, then?"

"I don't know. We left them this morning on the beach. They said they wanted to watch the sunrise."

"And what about us? What did we do?" He was curious, like a child wanting to know the end of a story.

"We came back here." She studied her long, electric-blue nails impatiently.

"And did we make love?"

She nodded.

"Well, how was it?" He was anxious, waiting for her approval.

"Oh, okay. You weren't too good," she answered coldly. "You were too fast."

"Oh, well, let me show you something now." He

moved toward her, but she rolled out of his grasp.

"No, I don't want to, and besides, you smell. Go take a shower."

"You're really Little Miss **Charm** School, aren't you?"

She gave him the finger and then jumped off the bed to collect her clothes.

Clive pulled himself up and moved toward the bathroom. He needed a drink, but more than that, he wanted to get away from this girl. It was his own fault. He shouldn't mess around with such young stuff. It always got him into trouble. Jason had lectured him enough about it.

"You have to curb your appetites, Clive, for girls, rich food, drugs. I have helped you, but I cannot always protect you." Yet Jason always had, and Clive believed in his heart that he always would.

He stepped into the shower and turned on the hot water. The heat and force of the water woke him and brought his mind back to Key West. He remembered why he was there in the first place.

It had been Billy's idea. Billy had caught the gig of a new young group, "like Buffett and the Coral Reefers," he had told him, and they had flown down to see the act at Miller's Back Yard. Muffy had been one of the groupies hanging around and she believed Clive when he told her he could put her in show business. It was the only truthful thing he had told her all night. If he wanted to, he could make her a star, but the girl was too young even to know who he was.

"Do you remember what you said to me last night?" She had come into the bathroom.

"What's that, luv?" Clive shouted over the water.

"That you were in the music business, or something, and, you know, you could get me a job maybe. I mean, what do you do exactly?"

Clive turned off the water and pulled back the shower curtain. He could smell the dope. She was standing in the doorway dressed in short jean cut-offs, a pink T-shirt with GET LAID stenciled across the front, and now Clive remembered her. The past twelve hours were coming back to him in a rush of regrets.

"Give me a hit of that, luv, will ya?"

"Stop calling me luv!" She handed him the joint. "You English talk like a bunch of queers!"

Clive took several quick hits and returned the cigarette, holding the smoke in his lungs for a moment.

"Well, what about it?" She moved around him and sat down on the toilet seat. "What do you do? Are you a talent scout or something? Sherri and me have this routine, you know; we sing one of Buffett's songs, 'Cheeseburger in Paradise,' and do a little soft-shoe disco number."

"Soft-shoe disco number," Clive mumbled, unpacking his shaving gear.

"Do you want me to find Sherri? Maybe we could sing for you, or something."

Clive glanced at her. She had the eager and accommodating look of a cocker spaniel.

"Well, I'm not exactly a talent scout," he confessed. "I'm a music producer." He caught himself before saying "luv." "And Billy...Billy's my scout in the U.S. He finds me talent, I produce the shows in Europe."

"Europe? I don't want to go to Europe." She

immediately lost interest. "I thought you had something to do with Nashville."

"Well, everyone in the music business has 'something' to do with Nashville . . . Muffy. But I'm not into music over here. Europe is my scene; you know, England, France, the Low Countries, all over, really. Eastern Europe as well, Bulgaria, Rumania. I'm doing an outdoor gig in Belgrade this summer."

"Bulgaria? I don't even know where that is," she shouted, disgusted.

"Well, I'll draw you a map, how's that?" He finished shaving and went back into the room. Now he had fixed her. Never mind all the English groups he had produced, the American punk-rockers he had discovered. Now she thought he was a European weirdo. She'd wander off in a few minutes and he promised himself, not for the first time, never to do this again.

"Why don't you call your friend Sherri, see what she's up to?" Kids her age, he had found, always got lonely for their girl friends.

"Yeah, okay." But the telephone rang before she could reach it.

"It's Billy," he said, brushing past her. "Run along, luv; I'll remember you to the Danube." He picked up the receiver as she disappeared, and said, "Hello, old son!" But it wasn't Billy. The call was from overseas, from a large house in a small corner of Great Britain. It was Adams, telling him it was time to come home.

In the huge, silent country mansion, Adams hung

up the telephone and left the library, moving quickly through the empty rooms, then upstairs and past the Portrait Hall, taking the back stairs to the room that had been especially prepared for him.

Adams slipped into the bedroom, glancing at the monitoring equipment to see that everything was in order, then went through the glass partition and closer to the bed. He was beginning to breathe with difficulty, long, labored breaths, but that was the best Adams could expect.

"They have all been notified, sir."

"Good. Very well done, Adams." He spoke slowly, his rasping voice barely a whisper. "Is everything ready?"

"Yes, sir."

"Then good night, Adams. We'll start tomorrow."

"Very good, sir." Adams paused a moment, and then asked, "Are you sure you'll be able? Perhaps Harry can take the Rolls himself . . . ?"

"No!" Now he was angry. "I must be the one who brings her home to Ravenshurst."

"Yes, sir. I have the medication required, but it will only give you a few hours."

"That is time enough, Adams."

"Very good, sir." Adams lowered the lights so he could sleep, then closed the door and went back into the empty house.

Now only the cat was awake. The small white feline ran soundlessly through the sixteenth-century mansion, slipping through the open doors, running from room to room, past the cool, still swimming pool, down to the Grand Hall, and into the library.

John Coyne

And there in front of the fireplace, in the warmth of the dying embers, she settled down, made herself comfortable on the hearth, stretched and cuddled up to sleep in the soft, warm glowing light.

Chapter Seven

THE TRIUMPH BONNEVILLE RACED through Charing
and into the English countryside with Maggie
clinging to Pete, her arms wrapped tightly around
his waist.

She looked ahead. The road was clear for several
miles, a two-lane country highway that followed the
hills toward Canterbury. Under her tight grip, she
could feel Pete's body tense as he shifted the bike
from third into fourth, and lean forward against the
wind. He would race all the way, she knew, and she
quickly tapped him on the shoulder.

"I thought I was giving directions," she shouted
over the engine and the rush of wind.

Pete nodded, then gestured, "Which way?"

"There!" Maggie pointed impulsively toward an unmarked side road that left the highway at an angle and disappeared over the crest of a small hill.

"We'll get lost," he protested. "I don't know this part of Kent."

Maggie shrugged. "It doesn't matter. There's always a village at the end of these country lanes; we can ask directions."

Pete nodded and turned the bike onto the narrow lane, a thin black ribbon of tarmac between stone walls and green hedges. He knew what Maggie was doing: keeping him off the main road so he wouldn't speed. He smiled to himself and then, just for an instant, as a way of reminding her who was driving, he raced the engine and flipped it into gear. The bike jumped forward, sprayed loose gravel, and tore ahead. Maggie screamed, but her alarm was muffled in her helmet.

He did keep the speed down, resisting the temptation to race through the back roads. He relaxed and drove slowly, letting Maggie choose directions when they reached a junction.

They wandered for almost an hour through the sprawling network of narrow lanes, through small villages, past farms and stone-walled estates, stopping only when the view was breathtaking or they came upon a flock of sheep crossing the road. It was a side of England he had thought no longer existed.

"I'm beginning to feel better," Maggie said at one point, when the road ahead was momentarily blocked with sheep. "I have this feeling that I've seen it all, or been here before."

"You have," said Pete, leaning back. He gestured

at the countryside: the thatched house down in the hollow, the green fields with a small stream crossing the land, and the flock of sheep on the road being herded by an old man and two golden collies. "This is a scene from a thousand postcards and British tourist calendars."

"No," she answered, resisting his easy explanation. "It's more than a familiar picture. I feel comfortable, that's all, as if I belong."

"Forget it, Mag. You're a southern California girl. All this rainy weather would drive you batty after a few months." He raised up on the seat, kick-started the bike and, before she could reply, spun the Triumph back onto the road. They shot ahead, dodged the last of the sheep, and turned into a tight corner.

The backroads were mostly deserted in the mid-morning hours, and Pete took over the highway, moving back and forth playfully, rolling the bike tight as he made a turn, then shooting out again into the middle of the tarmac.

Maggie dug her fingers into his side to caution him, but he was having too much fun. The bike handled beautifully and they took another tight country curve. He could feel Maggie's body resisting the turn. If she would only relax, he thought, it would be easier to drive. He leaned hard to the right, against the wind, and they raced into the turn.

Maggie had shut her eyes. She never even saw the enormous Rolls-Royce that filled the road and blocked the way. Pete tried to stop, then realized he couldn't and jerked the wheel left so they would miss the car. The wheels tore into the soft shoulder, then slid out from beneath them, and Maggie and Pete tumbled over into the grassy field beyond the low hedge.

Maggie knew she would not die, and knew she would not be seriously hurt. She did not know why, but when she landed on the marshy ground and tumbled forward, keeping her arms and legs tucked close to her body, she only worried about Pete. It was he who was in danger, not she.

She stopped tumbling and for a moment lay back in the soft grass. It was so silent, not a sound, and it was peaceful, the way she imagined death must be. Then she heard a car door slam, and another door, then voices and someone running toward them through the wet leaves.

"Are you okay, Mag?" Pete knelt beside her, taking off her helmet. His face was white and his hands trembled, but he was all right. She felt immensely better.

"Yes, I think so." She tried to sit up.

"Lie still and don't move." It was another man's voice, a strong and authoritative English voice that Maggie instantly obeyed.

Pete looked around. Two men were rushing to them. One was dressed in a gray chauffeur's uniform, the second was tall and thin, and dressed in a three-piece Harris tweed suit. He came directly to Maggie's side and knelt down across from Pete.

He had wonderful soft-blue eyes, Maggie saw immediately, eyes that suggested he was older than he seemed.

"Where does it hurt?" he asked softly, and moved his hand along her leg to feel her knees and ankles.

Then he looked at her. The smile on his face was comforting. She felt suddenly at ease.

"All over, I'm afraid." She tried to laugh, but it hurt her sides.

"Try and sit up, Mag," Pete urged.

"One moment, please," the man ordered. "How many fingers do you see?" He spread the fingers of his left hand before her eyes. His fingers were long and fine, and on his index finger was a silver signet ring. The ring was too large and had twisted around, giving her a glimpse of its odd insignia.

"Eleven or twelve," she answered, smiling. On her own, she began to struggle to stand. The cold ground had dampened her jeans uncomfortably.

The man smiled, seeing that she was okay, and helped Pete pull her to her feet.

"I think you are a very lucky girl," he said. "And you, too, young man." He glanced at Pete for an instant, then looked back immediately at Maggie.

"But the bike wasn't." Pete walked to the Triumph. The chauffeur had already picked it out of the hedge and Pete could see the front wheel was bent.

"Well, at the moment all that matters is that you are in one piece," the man answered. He bent for Maggie's helmet and handed it to her. She looked up and smiled just as he frowned and the color left his face.

"Are you all right, sir?" Maggie touched his arm.

"Why, yes." He smiled again. "All the excitement, I guess." He slipped his hands into his pocket and pulled out a gold pill box. "The old ticker," he explained, forcing a smile, then turned their attention to the chauffeur. "How is it, Harry?"

Harry dumped the bike into the grass and walked toward them. "I'll have to get someone to attend to it, sir." He shook his head, and said apologetically to Pete, "You were on the wrong side of the road, sir."

Pete raised his hands, indicating that he understood. "Yeah, I know." He was angry for letting it happen and he didn't need the chauffeur to remind him whose fault it was.

"Let's go home, then," the English gentleman suggested. "I don't live far from here. You can relax, and we'll decide what to do about your transport problem."

Pete backed off. "Oh, no, I'll stay here. I'd rather not leave the bike unguarded." He glanced toward the road. "Someone will rip it off."

"Oh, my dear chap, the bike will be perfectly all right, I assure you. This isn't California, you know. Come along." He turned toward the Rolls, expecting them to follow.

"You really don't have to take us home with you," Maggie said, looking back and forth between Pete and the Englishman.

"Good heavens!" The man paused. "Do you really think I could leave you stranded?" He sounded slightly put off, then immediately his voice softened and he added nicely: "Please, you would do me a great honor. After all, it was my Rolls that caused you all these problems." He smiled at Maggie, the same warm, attentive smile that again, inexplicably, made her feel secure, the same way Pete sometimes did.

She looked at Pete, hoping he wouldn't insist on staying with the bike. "It will be okay," she ventured. "Who's going to take it in that wrecked condition?"

"We'll drive into the village and have a man from the garage come out and fetch it, how's that?" the gentleman said. He was standing beside the Rolls, leaning slightly against it for support.

Pete looked once more at the bike. "Okay, if you think it's safe." Then he went to get the saddlebags and Maggie walked up the slight incline to the parked car.

"My name is Jason Mountolive," the gentleman said, when they had settled themselves inside the huge back seat of the Rolls.

"Pete Danner." Pete reached out and shook the man's hand. "And this is Maggie Walsh."

"Are you on holiday then?" Mountolive asked as Harry turned the car around on the narrow road, turning it back toward where they had come from.

"No... Well, yes... kind of..." Maggie laughed, embarrassed at her own confusion. "You see," she said, starting over, "I have a job in London but it doesn't officially start until next week. At least, that's what we think now, but it's too complicated to go into." She gestured toward Pete, including him, and said, "So we're taking time off to see your beautiful countryside."

Pete leaned forward and added, "She wanted to see where her English blood comes from."

"You're English, then?" Mountolive raised his eyebrows and focused his attention on her, though his eyes had rarely left her since they met.

"Just on my mother's side, and not very directly. Her family has been in America for generations." She was embarrassed, passing herself off as English.

"Coming home then, were you? And here you were almost half killed by the locals for your trouble."

Pete leaned forward again. "Look, I'm sorry. It really was my fault."

"No, no," Mountolive protested, his tone harsher and more insistent. "I blame my driver. He was daydreaming. He should have seen you on the bike."

Maggie looked up and saw the driver's back tense and his grip tighten on the steering wheel, but Mountolive kept talking, oblivious of his employee. "We don't have much traffic down here in the country and our drivers become very lackadaisical. But let us not spend our time arguing who was responsible. I am still concerned about Miss Walsh." He looked again at Maggie, almost fondly. His intense interest was beginning to make her nervous.

"Really, I'm okay." She had said it before, but now she wasn't so sure. To hide her sudden misgivings she smiled at Mountolive, but this time he did not respond. He seemed tired, and she saw him slip his hand again into his suit pocket and take out the small gold pill box. She looked away, not wanting to embarrass him with her staring.

The Rolls slowed as they pulled into a small village and stopped at a garage.

"Isn't this lovely?" Maggie exclaimed, looking down the narrow street with thatched-roof houses on either side. "How did we miss this village, Pete?" she asked.

"It's off the main bypass," Mountolive interjected, recovering from his momentary silence.

"I'll just have a word with Wade, sir," the chauffeur explained and opened the driver's door.

"Very good, Harry."

Maggie turned quickly to Mountolive, catching him staring intensely at her.

"This is really very kind of you," she said.

"Nonsense. Americans are the kindest people on earth. I look upon this as a small chance to repay some of the marvelous hospitality I have always been shown in your country." He kept smiling at Maggie and she had to turn away to break eye contact.

"How old is this Rolls, Mr. Mountolive?" Pete asked, missing the silent exchange.

"Over forty years old, Mr. Danner." Mountolive seemed to have shrunk into the deep back seat, and his heavy suit seemed too bulky, but his voice was strong and powerful. "This is the Rolls-Royce P-Three, built in 1937. Are you a connoisseur of fine automobiles?"

"Just a fan. I'm afraid I'll never be able to afford anything quite like this."

"Well, there aren't many left today. I purchased this car the year it was made. It was one of the first cars that Henry Royce did not work on personally, and only a few years later they changed the color from red to black. This is now considered one of the finest luxury cars of all time. Not as fast, I might add, as the Continental, but a much more delightful

car in which to travel. I prefer it above all your
super-luxury cars of today."

"Do you travel much, Mr. Mountolive?" Maggie
asked, making conversation.

He shook his head and again she saw his eyes
cloud up with fatigue. "No, Miss Walsh, I rarely
leave home anymore. But once..."—his smile had
returned, only it was much weaker now—"but
once," he went on, "I traveled a great deal. I was
much younger then." He touched her knee. His
hand was light and fragile on her leg. "I was as
young as you, my dear."

Maggie laughed nervously. "Oh, Mr. Mountolive, you're hardly about to be confined to a
wheelchair. Why, I think you look quite handsome," she added flirtatiously. And she did. She
liked his dignified, reserved manner.

"Everything is arranged, sir," Harry said, coming
back to the car. "Wade will collect the bike and have
a look at it."

"Thank you, Harry," Mountolive replied.

Pete glanced out the window. He could see the
mechanic in the doorway of his garage, a short,
thick-necked man with his hands on a rag, but when
the mechanic noticed Pete watching him he turned
away abruptly and disappeared into the garage.

"Do you think he can fix a new Triumph?" Pete
asked, suddenly concerned about the mechanic.

"Oh, yes, sir," Harry replied. "Wade can fix any
sort of machine. He's a real genius with motorcars."

"I wouldn't worry, Mr. Danner," Mountolive
added. "Wade will have it in proper shape in no
time. Now how about some tea? Surely you can stop

that long. In this country everything stops for tea."

Maggie sighed and felt immensely better. The bike would be fixed and they could soon be on their way again. It would only take a few extra hours, no time at all. Everything was all right.

"Sure," she replied enthusiastically. "I think that would be just perfect."

Harry drove the Rolls-Royce through the small village. The houses were in perfect condition, the roofs newly thatched, the sidewalks swept clear. It looked like a storybook village, she thought, and wished they would pass a pedestrian so she could see how the local women dressed. But they passed no one.

Then they were out of town, not taking the main road but branching off immediately and following a single lane that went uphill behind the village into a small forest of evergreens. They crossed a stone bridge and drove into a meadow filled with sheep. Harry picked up speed only to slow again at another junction.

"For a small country," Maggie joked, "you certainly have an elaborate network of roads. How do strangers find their way to your place?"

"Oh, well, you see, we don't have many strangers here in our small world."

The Rolls swung off the country road and stopped abruptly before a set of huge iron gates. Harry tapped lightly on the horn, and through the front window Maggie saw someone running to swing open the gates and let them in.

They followed a curving drive now and crossed an open meadow. In the fields to the right, a young man was riding a chestnut horse, and leading a brown mare. He moved away from the driveway as the car passed.

"Afternoon, Mister Mountolive, sir," he called as the car rolled swiftly by. Mountolive waved and nodded.

The drive turned and went directly up toward the house and Maggie could see it now, dominating the crest of the hill. It was a large stone mansion, three stories high. The lawns surrounding the house were clipped, and cleared of trees and bushes, so that the grass rolled up to the massive house like a wave of cold sea water crashing against a stone fortress.

Maggie gasped at the unexpected sight of the huge house. Simple pleasure filled her face and her eyes flashed. Pete smiled, happy for her. And, he had to admit, he wouldn't mind seeing the interior of a real Elizabethan manor house himself.

He looked at Mountolive. "Is this all yours?"

"It's not much," he answered drily, "but it's home."

The Rolls-Royce stopped before the front doors and Harry jumped out quickly and came around to open the rear door before Pete could move. He even reached inside and picked up the saddlebags and took them from the car.

"Thank you, Harry." It made Pete uneasy to have his luggage carried by a man not much older than himself.

Just before Maggie stepped out, she turned to say something to Mountolive. His pale face was now distorted, as if he were in pain.

"Are you all right?" she asked quickly.

"Yes, yes, I'm fine. Please go ahead." He

attempted to wave, but let his hand drop to his lap. "I will join you in a few minutes."

Maggie nodded uncertainly, then stepped from the Rolls as a black Doberman came racing across the lawns toward the car. It charged between Harry and Pete and jumped at Maggie who instinctively lurched back, falling into the rear seat.

"Down! Set!" Mountolive had pulled himself up to the edge of the seat, bracing his arm against the door as he shouted at the dog. There was nothing fragile about his voice, and the dog reluctantly backed off, confused at the order, and sat and looked passively at Maggie.

"I'm terribly sorry about this, Miss Walsh. You're perfectly safe." Then he slipped back into the deep seat, as if hiding himself from view, and added, almost in a whisper, "Adams will take care of you. Please make yourselves at home."

Harry stepped between Maggie and the car and closed the back door. Then he went to the driver's side and started the Rolls, driving the huge car slowly out of the entrance and around the corner, leaving them alone in front of the manor house.

Chapter Eight

"WELL," SAID MAGGIE, "I guess this is what you call crashing up in style." She stepped back from the house to take it all in. "It's sixteenth-century, isn't it?"

"Yes, exact except for those hipped roofs and those mullion-and-transom crossed windows." He pointed toward the second and third stories of the house.

"When do you think it was built?"

"Any time after 1580, I'd guess. We'll have to ask Mountolive. This house has probably been in his family since the sixteenth century. Let's go look inside."

Maggie glanced uneasily at the dog that still sat on the grass beside the horseshoe drive.

"Will he let me?"

The dog's tongue was hanging out and he sat panting. He looked up at them both, then turned his head away, uninterested.

"Let's go," Pete urged, "before he changes his mind." He took her by the arm and they circled around the dog and stepped through the front door into the foyer.

The entrance hall was large and high-ceilinged, with a marble fireplace and a carved wooden staircase to the second floor. They moved inside slowly, both awed by the elaborate entranceway. "Look at this," Maggie whispered, her hand touching the delicate-shaped acanthus flowers that were carved into the panels of the staircase.

Pete went closer to the balustrade and studied the wood.

"I've seen this kind of carving only a few times before. Once at the Ham House in Surrey, and again at Sudbury Hall in Derbyshire." He looked up at the high ceiling. "See, Maggie, how perfectly it's done? Those leaf fronds and flower-sags? It was incredibly difficult to create that effect. The leaf tendrils were modeled in plaster on a real leaf, while the plaster was still soft. Then the mold was twisted into position before the plaster had set." Pete stood back, taking in the full scope of the foyer and the opulent staircase. "This room," he said after a moment, "is right out of the 1500's. There has been no modernization. It's a perfect gem. I wonder if the British National Trust even knows it exists."

Maggie was only half listening. She had moved

toward a doorway and peeped inside. "Who are we looking for, anyway?"

"A guy named Adams." Pete set the saddlebags and helmets by the fireplace and followed Maggie into the next room.

"God, look at this!" she exclaimed. The room was smaller and more intimate, and there was a fire in the stone fireplace and decanters were set out on a glass coffee table. "He must be expecting company," Maggie whispered, looking everywhere at once, trying to take it all in so she would have firsthand knowledge of how a wealthy English gentleman decorated his house.

But there was almost too much to see: gilded chairs carved with dolphins and covered with rose-red satin brocade; a ceiling plastered with wreaths of flowers and fruit; tapestried walls; wooden bookcases filled with leather volumes; stone busts of Roman figures; a marble fireplace; deep-cushioned sofas flanking the coffee table of drinks.

"Do you think there's more?" Maggie asked.

"Sure. The Grand Hall, or dining room, would be this way." He pointed toward heavy blue velvet curtains that covered one doorway.

"Is that where tea is served?"

"Not for us; I think they make Americans eat in the kitchen." Pete pushed the curtain aside and they stepped into the Grand Hall.

An oak table stretched the length of the long, narrow room. There was another fireplace, with a white cat stretched lazily before the blaze. Wood paneling decorated the lower half of the room and the paneling and the stone walls above were covered with paintings.

"Is that a real Picasso?" Maggie asked, pointing out one painting.

"Are you serious? There isn't a fake in this house, I'm sure. Look, he's even got a Canaletto and a Titian. The least expensive thing this Mountolive owns is his '37 Rolls."

"Do you think he'd mind us snooping through his house?"

"We're not snooping; we're looking for Adams." Pete kept walking.

"Watch it, Pete!" Maggie caught his arm. "You almost stepped on the cat."

The white cat had leaped off the hearth and slipped between Maggie's legs, arching its back against her leather boots.

"She likes you," Pete said.

"Isn't she lovely?" Maggie knelt and gently stroked the cat, who purred and neatly licked Maggie's hand.

"Come on! Let's find this Adams."

Maggie stood and the cat ran off, leaving Maggie to follow Pete through another hallway and into a kitchen, a room bright with afternoon sunlight. The kitchen, too, was empty, except for several gray cats sitting on the windowsill.

"They can't have gone very far," Pete noted, pointing to pots simmering on the stove and chopped vegetables on the wood table.

"Isn't this lovely!" It was a large, old-fashioned country kitchen with ham and sausages hanging from the ceiling beams, and another fireplace in the corner of the room.

"And you'd like it back at our place in the Valley, wouldn't you?" Pete grinned.

"I'd love it!"

"Adams?" Pete called out. When no one answered, he said again, this time with a British accent, "Adams? Oh, I say, Adams, are you there?"

"Don't." Maggie giggled. "Someone will hear you."

"Who? Christ, this place is a tomb."

They left the kitchen just as the Rolls pulled up behind the house. Only the house cats, sunning themselves on the windows, saw Harry reach inside and very slowly help Mountolive out, gently placing his feet on the ground, first the right, then the left.

In the foyer, Maggie found another door and moved toward it.

"We should wait," Pete cautioned, worried that they might be taking too much liberty.

"Come on, live dangerously." She waved, and led the way through a doorway in the back wall of the entrance hall. Pete followed reluctantly through a short passageway and onto a balcony overlooking an indoor swimming pool. It was a large chamber lit by a skylight, a beautiful room decorated with soft pink tiles, plush blue-velvet lounge chairs, and an open aerie. Small tropical birds flew across the wide, warm pool, soaring up to perch on the iron framework of the skylight.

"This place is marvelous!" Maggie exclaimed, taking it all in. "I wonder what this guy does for a living!"

"Whatever it is, he's doing it right." Pete stared down at the still water. "What's that?" He pointed to a huge mosaic that shimmered on the pool's bottom.

"I don't know, but I noticed that Mountolive was wearing a ring with the same design. It must be the family crest."

"But what does it represent?"

"It looks like a bird—see the shape of the wings, and the head?"

"Miss Walsh!" A distant voice called.

Maggie's head jerked up.

"It must be tea time," Pete whispered, and they turned back, stepping through the passageway and reentering the foyer.

"Miss Walsh?"

Maggie spun around. On the second floor, against the banister, an English nurse stared down at her. The woman wore a white uniform with a starched veil that concealed her hair, and a fresh white apron. She was a plain-looking woman in her fifties and she did not smile or look pleased.

"Hello." Maggie smiled apologetically. "Excuse us, but we're looking for Mr. Adams."

"I am Nurse Adams," the woman said flatly. "You must be Miss Walsh and Mr. . . . ."

"Danner. Peter Danner," he answered quickly. The nurse came down the stairs and wordlessly picked up their saddlebags.

"Would you follow me, please?"

Maggie glanced at Pete, who shrugged and indicated that they might as well. They climbed the curving staircase to the second floor, then walked along a hallway of bedrooms.

"Wait a minute," Maggie protested, following the nurse into a room. "There must be some mistake."

The nurse set the bag on the double bed, a question in her eyes. "Yes?" she asked.

"We're just staying for a cup of tea," Maggie explained.

"I was told your motorcycle was beyond repair."

Her small, taut-lipped mouth curved into a frown.

"No, they're going to fix it," Pete spoke up. "We might rent a car in the meantime."

Adams shook her head and allowed herself a wry smile. "You won't find one locally, I'm afraid." Then, as if issuing an order, she said, "This is your room."

"There's a garage in the village," Maggie added quickly, stepping closer, trying to make her point more forcefully.

"Miss Walsh," the nurse said calmly, "you are not in Los Angeles. Hardly anyone in these parts has cause to hire a car."

"Terrific," Pete said.

"Mr. Mountolive's chauffeur suggested he might take you both into the nearest town tomorrow," the nurse said, turning down the blankets. "There you will be accommodated. At this time of the year everything closes early." She stepped back from the bed and smiled gently at Maggie. "If this room is not to your liking, I can show you another..."

"Come on, honey, we can rough it here for a night," Pete said, looking around. It was a cozy room, warmed by a burning fire, and the bed had a canopy.

"Thank you, Nurse Adams," Maggie answered. "This room is just fine."

The nurse moved toward the door, saying as she closed it behind her, "No doubt you would like to rest after your unpleasant accident. You will not be disturbed." She smiled thinly, and disappeared.

Maggie took off her jacket and then sat on the edge of the bed and jerked off her boots. She stretched out on the bed, warming herself, glad to be off the back of the bike for awhile.

Pete was still standing in the middle of the bedroom. He had taken off his jacket, but seemed to be lost in thought. Maggie swung off the bed and went to him.

"You okay?" she asked.

"Yes, just trying to get warm." He was frowning. "How did she know we were from L.A., Mag?"

"I don't know. Maybe Mountolive told her."

"No," said Pete. "We didn't tell Mountolive. He knew it, though. He said the bike would be okay because England was safer than California."

"Oh, Pete, be serious. We're obviously Americans, and he's obviously been around. You always say you can tell a New Yorker as soon as you spot one at an L.A. restaurant like Ma Maison. Maybe he knows the California type when he sees it."

Before she could say anything more, he picked her up, handling her small body easily.

"I'm not the 'California type,'" he growled. "I'm really an English lord, and you're my scullery maid."

She laughed, then leaned her head against his chest as he carried her back to the soft down bed.

He began to undress her, and she sat quietly while he slipped off her leather jacket and pulled up her white sweater. There was another layer of clothes underneath, a thinner sweater and a cotton shirt.

"What is this?" he asked, as the discarded clothes piled up on the floor. "You're wearing all your luggage!"

She peeled off the final T-shirt herself. It was her favorite, the one with UPPITY WOMEN UNITE printed across the front. "Sorry, my lord," she said. "At least I'm not wearing a bra!"

He nodded. He so loved her breasts; after all his time with her, and his familiarity with her body, her breasts still thrilled him. They were not unusual, not large or particularly full. They were like a young girl's, slight and immature and tender. He was struck always at how tender they were, and how innocent and shy she became without clothes.

He pulled off his boots and dropped them beside the bed. Then he lifted up her hips as he pulled down her tight jeans.

"Maggie, I don't believe this!" She was wearing long winter leggings.

"Well, it gets cold on that bike!" she protested. "Never mind, I'll take them off."

"No wonder our sex life is so complicated. Just getting you naked takes so much time."

"Don't be such a smart-ass." He sat on the edge of the bed, slowly unbuttoning his flannel shirt as he watched her. She was busy with her hair, untwisting her long, single braid and combing it out so it hung loosely down the length of her back.

"There," she said, smiling at him, pleased with the effect she had created. She knew, the way women do, when she looked truly lovely.

He motioned her toward him, but she shook her head in a small show of defiance. Not yet, her eyes told him. She wanted him to enjoy the sight of her and she wanted to see that look of admiration in his slate eyes. He was always so cool and controlled and would never let a burst of emotions indicate his feelings. She knew it was a California thing, that way of being laid back. But when he was with her, watching her hair and her body, she wanted to see him react simply, with delight on his face. It gave her a sense of power, and she needed that sense of supremacy to make sex good for her.

He had finished undressing and slipped into bed, tucking the blankets and sheets around his waist. She went to the bed and pulled away the blankets, exposing his body. She smiled down at him. He knew his body excited her, the slim hips and long legs. His body, she had told him, had been the first thing that attracted her to him.

She bent over and kissed him, her loose hair falling across his body. She kept kissing him, moving down his body. He reached down to pull her up to him, but she shook her head.

"I'm not finished," she said, stopping him.

"Oh," he laughed, pleased by her sudden boldness.

She was blocking out everything from her mind but the touch of his skin, the feeling of his muscles, tense under her long fingers, the palms of her hands. Then she stretched out beside him, accepting the pleasure of his hand while he stirred her passion.

Now she lay back, letting Pete gently and slowly pull her through a tanglewood of fears. This was always the moment when her mind resisted, fought and would not let go. She had never been able to reach an orgasm, had never been able to break through her strange need to protect herself, to maintain control rather than float free on a tide of passion. She had never felt safe enough, not with any lover, not even with Pete. A small cup of fear always spilled out, seeping through her body like a deadening poison and spoiling her final moment.

She closed her eyes and tried to let Pete take over, but she was really waiting for the fear to wipe out her pleasure. She knew the moment. She knew how her passion fathered his and fed off it, strengthened and then roared through her body, only to be stifled by her strange malady.

She waited for her body to fail her, to pull away from the heat and warmth of love. She felt the pain, enjoyed the luxury of it, prayed that Pete would keep at her. If she only had enough time, she thought. If only he could go on endlessly, it would break down her resistance. She cried out, and he hesitated.

"No, no," she begged, "please don't stop." She stretched her arms to seize him, to squeeze him against her, his body and hers wet with sweat. She raked her hands across his back. Her fingernails were drawing blood but she couldn't stop herself.

It was happening, she realized. She had gone through the wall of her caution and now, as if picked up by a cresting wave, she tumbled forward, her body out of control. It shook and she hung on desperately to him, held on as it tore through her limbs, exploding and leaving her exhausted and gasping for breath.

"My God," she whispered, clinging to Pete. "It happened, darling. I think it happened! I mean, God, *something* happened!"

He kissed her on the eyes and let her come down slowly, not interrupting her pleasure, but feeling immensely proud.

"Oh, God," she leaned away and brushed her hair

from her face. "That was so beautiful. Do you think we can buy this bed from Mountolive? I want to have it bronzed."

Pete nuzzled his nose against her. "It wasn't this bed or the canopy or, I hate to admit it, even me. I didn't do anything special or different. It was you. You deserve the credit."

"Then what took me so long?"

"I don't know, but I could tell there was something different this time. These things are unpredictable, Maggie. Maybe it's the romantic surroundings."

"I do feel comfortable here . . ."

"Who wouldn't, with all this luxury?"

"No, it's something else. I mean, that's part of it, sure, but there is something more about the place. I just have a feeling . . . I'm glad Mountolive asked us to stay."

"Of course you are." Pete slipped his arm around her. "And so am I."

Chapter Nine

THEY SLEPT SOUNDLY UNTIL the helicopter woke them. The propellers blew smoke down the chimney and shook the windows as the copter settled to a landing on the lawn.

Maggie sat up on her elbows, unsure for a moment where she was.

Pete had already gotten out of bed, grabbed a towel off the rack in the bathroom and moved to the window, parting the heavy curtains as he looked down at the lawn.

The helicopter was less than a hundred yards from the house, the long propeller blades dipping as the power cut off and it came to a stop. Two Dobermans had raced out to charge the copter and now they stood barking at the whirling blades.

"Seems like we aren't the only guests," Pete said over his shoulder. He could see the house servants driving a golf cart toward the parked copter.

"Who?" Maggie was interested, but not enough to leave the warm bed.

"Not sure." He moved closer to the window. The propellers had stopped and the side doors of the copter were being pulled open. "It looks like two couples," he reported. "And they're dressed for a formal dinner." When the power was cut off, the dogs summoned up their courage. But when they charged the passengers, the men raised their hands and the dogs backed off, whimpering as they retreated.

"Young or old?" Maggie asked.

"Both. There's a white-haired man with a limp, and a blonde who's not bad-looking."

"Oh, yeah? Get away from that window," Maggie ordered, then added, "They'll see you."

"No, they won't."

"Are we still being watched?" Karl asked, turning his back to the mansion.

"Yes, I believe so." Jacques nervously took off his leather gloves and put them back on again.

"Who is he?" Karl asked. The flight from Gatwick had left him jumpy.

"Well, he's very pretty," said Maria, "whoever he is."

"Another special gift from Jason, darling?" Barbara came around the helicopter to join the others.

"Arthur?" Karl asked, turning to the houseman

who was unloading the luggage. "When is the American due?"

Arthur paused and straightened before replying. "She's here now, sir."

"Already?" Jacques reacted. "Has she seen him yet?"

"I really wouldn't know, sir." He waited a moment, as if for more questions.

"Who's the man on the second floor?" asked Maria.

"Apparently he is the young lady's, er . . . friend, madame."

Barbara smiled wryly at Maria. "Bad luck, darling." Then she turned back to Arthur. "Did Mr. Jackson arrive yet?"

"No, madame, not yet." And he reached into the helicopter and lifted out a case of Roederer Cristal champagne and carried it up to the house himself. The others followed behind.

"Oh, it's cold!" Maria tightened her white sable about her neck, then slipped her arm into Karl's, whispering as they walked, "Can't we get this business over with tonight?"

"Oh, that reminds me." Karl stopped abruptly and shouted back to the pilot of the helicopter, "Nine sharp! Sunday morning!"

The pilot nodded and pulled the copter doors closed.

"Sunday?" Maria shook her head. "How dreary, darling."

"We cannot just arrive, say hello to him, and depart," he answered in his thick German accent. "Perhaps you are not as fond of Jason as you profess . . ."

Maria looked up and smiled at Karl. "Well, if the truth be known, Karl, I am a lot fonder of you."

"And why should I believe you?" Karl chuckled.

"Well, have I ever lied to you?"

"Yes, Maria, darling, you have," he replied, and there was no longer any humor in his voice.

Pete watched the helicopter lift off. It rose quickly, turned and shot across the top of the house, again billowing smoke into the bedroom. Then he turned and walked back to the bed.

"This is too much," Maggie said. She was sitting up with the blankets and sheets wrapped around her waist. "This house, this bed. Old Miss What's-Her-Face, and now a helicopter dropping dinner guests on the lawn."

Peter stretched out across the bed. "And we still haven't had our tea."

"But you've had me." Maggie leaned over and kissed him on his lips.

"Yes, I had you," he whispered.

"When are you going to do it again?" she asked, her eyes flashing.

"Before the sun sets," he said, "I promise, but right now I'm taking a long, hot shower. My poor bones hurt from that tumble we took. Don't yours?"

"Oh, I guess so, but I feel so good, I just forgot." She fell back into the soft bed and curled the pillow into her arms.

Pete shook his head as he moved toward the bathroom. "I think I've created a sex fiend."

Unlike the rest of the sixteenth-century mansion, the bathroom was modern, designed with glass and chrome fixtures and bright lights. It was a large room with both a glass shower and a separate tub. Pete took two bath towels off the rack and placed them next to the shower, then opened the glass door and turned on the hot water, testing it before he stepped inside the stall.

He wanted it hot. Hot enough to ease his sore back and thigh muscles. In the morning he would still be sore, but the afternoon of love-making had made him relax. He smiled, remembering his pleasure, and stepped into the warm shower, closing the glass door securely behind him.

A bar of soap hung from the shower head and Pete lifted it off and lathered his body, ducking his head in and out of the concentrated spray, as the hot water steamed and fogged up the closed stall. The water was too hot, he realized, and he reached through the fog to turn it down, but as he spun the knob the hot water increased, steaming and burning him.

He swore and pressed himself up against the side of the stall and spun the knob the opposite way. But instead of spraying cold water, the shower head hissed and more hot water poured out. Frantic now, he twisted the knob back again to turn the water off completely, but it only spun loosely in his hand and the scalding water continued to jet into the stall, the torrent of scorching water burning his skin.

Pete pushed at the shower door, but the latch was stuck, and the door would not open. He shouted for Maggie but she didn't answer. He braced himself against the wall and tried to kick out the door, but there wasn't enough space for him to get leverage. He shouted louder for Maggie. The drain had backed up and a half-inch of water covered the floor, burning his toes and the soles of his feet.

"What's wrong?" Maggie cried out from the other side of the door. All she could see was steam pouring through the cracks.

"I can't get the damn door open!"

She grabbed the handle and pulled, but it wouldn't budge. Water was spilling out onto the floor of the bathroom now, and it was hot, too hot for her to stand in. Suddenly she was terrified, realizing that Pete had been trapped under that water for several minutes.

"Shut it *off*!" she yelled, pounding on the door with her fist.

"I can't! The knobs are broken!" He had gotten onto the small ledge at the bottom of the stall, clinging to the wall and keeping out of the full force of the jetting water. He tried the knobs again; they spun loosely in his hand. "Damn!" he shouted.

The water at the bottom of the stall had risen to the ledge, lapping at his feet and burning his toes. The rubber mat now floated freely in the backed-up water, and he carefully slid down the wall of the shower and picked it up. He could hear Maggie still struggling with the door handle.

"Maggie," he yelled, "get back. I'm going to break this goddamn door."

He raised the mat over his head and shoulders, then stepped under the scalding water and charged the shower door. The glass shattered and Pete stumbled out and fell to the floor, bleeding from a dozen cuts. The water spilled out onto the bathroom floor, and he rolled away violently to escape it, leaving his blood smeared across the tiles.

"Son of a bitch!" he swore, stumbling to his feet.

Maggie stepped around the tide of hot water and reached inside the shower to turn off the faucets.

"You turned it the wrong way!" she yelled accusingly, trembling from the violent incident.

"Listen!" Pete pointed a finger toward the shower. "I turned those knobs every way. Nothing worked." He grabbed a white towel and pressed it against his cut shoulder. "Goddamn English plumbing!"

"Pete, you're bleeding!" Maggie said, following him into the bedroom. "God, you could have killed yourself."

"I'll survive," he snapped, still angry.

"I'll go get some bandages." She picked up his white robe and wrapped it snugly around her. "Your back is full of cuts!"

"It's okay; they aren't deep."

"Never mind, you're bleeding all over the bedroom and besides, I'd better tell someone. We have to clean up this mess." She was out of the room before he could stop her.

She closed the door behind her and walked along the hall. At the top of the stairs she met a woman dressed in a black tank suit. She was barefooted and had a bath towel tossed over her shoulder. "Hello," she said, in faintly accented English, "it's nice to meet you." She extended her hand.

"Maggie Walsh," Maggie said.

"Yes, I know," the woman answered, openly studying Maggie. "You are very young, I think." She seemed surprised.

The inspection annoyed Maggie. "Please excuse me," she said, "I'm in a hurry." She started down the stairs but the woman followed, and Maggie said, to be polite, "We saw the pool earlier today; it's quite beautiful. Do you swim there often?"

"Yes, whenever I am at Ravenshurst." Her voice was soft and measured. "My name is Maria Gabrielli. I see you have not been told who I am." She seemed disappointed.

"Actually, Pete and I know no one; we only arrived this afternoon and Jason just told us to make ourselves at home."

"Yes, Jason is that way." She smiled. "Everything of his belongs to us, you know?"

"Pardon me?" Maggie frowned, wondering whether the woman was having trouble with her English.

The Italian woman gestured, taking in the whole house. "At our convenience, no?"

"Oh, yes, I see what you mean," Maggie smiled. They had reached the entranceway and Maggie turned toward the Grand Hall, but Maria stopped her, saying, "You should know, Signorina Walsh, that of us all, I am the one Jason loves the most. As a woman, I know that, and you would be foolish to try to interfere. Besides, you have your young man. Keep him and be satisfied." She was smiling, but there was no kindness in her voice. Then she turned and walked toward the door to the swimming pool.

Maggie stood a moment staring after her. She did not understand the woman. Was it just more bad English? Her confusion made her feel foolish, but more than that she was puzzled that this woman seemed to know something she didn't.

She turned away, still shaken, and went through the Grand Hall to the kitchen. At the kitchen door, she could hear voices. Thank goodness, she thought, at least the place wasn't as deserted as it had been earlier. She pushed open the door and saw the nurse sitting at the kitchen table talking to the household staff. But at the sight of her, Adams broke off abruptly and stared pointedly as she stood, framed in the doorway.

"I'm sorry."

"Can I help you, ma'am?" the cook asked from the far end of the table.

"Yes, please, do you have some antiseptic? We had an accident in the shower. Pete was cut..."

"Oh, dear!" The cook motioned toward the other end of the table. "Nurse Adams'll help you."

Adams was on her feet and moving to the first-aid cabinet near the windows. Maggie followed her, saying, "I'm awfully sorry. I'm afraid the glass door got smashed too."

Adams smiled and handed her a small bottle and bandages, answering, "It's perfectly all right. I'll send the maid to tidy it away. Can you manage for the moment?"

"Oh, sure... Well, thank you." She turned to leave.

"Mind how you go now," the cook called after her as Maggie hurried out, closing the door behind her.

The staff sat quietly, listening to her footsteps fade away in the house before they relaxed and looked back at Adams, waiting for her to tell them the news.

Chapter Ten

"THANK YOU, HONEY," PETE SAID. His cuts were bandaged, but he moved his arm with some stiffness. "A bike accident and a scalding shower, all in one day." He shook his head. "I'm lucky to be alive."

"Well, nothing else is going to happen; I'm taking care of you now." She kissed him softly on the cheek.

He picked up his shirt and, with Maggie's help, put it on. "I'm going to call that garage right now and see how they're doing with the bike. Come with me, will you? I'm liable to get lost trying to find the first floor."

"Sure." Maggie slipped her arm around his waist

and they went downstairs to the foyer. "This way," she said, heading off to the right.

"Why?"

"I don't know. I just have a feeling the phone is that way, in the library, that's all." She stopped in front of one of the oak doors and pointed.

Pete looked quizzically at her, shook his head, and knocked softly on the door. When no one answered, he pushed it open and peeped inside.

Maggie slid by him to look for herself. As she had suspected, it was the library. She had seen too many illustrated books on English manor houses not to know where the library was likely to be. A small fire was burning, but the room was lit by the afternoon sun and two lamps. It was a charming room, warm and inviting, and walled with old books, more paintings and portraits, and heavy leather furniture. Over the fireplace hung two shotguns, the wooden stocks beautifully polished to a fine gleam.

"May I help?" someone asked.

The voice startled her and she looked around the door. Behind the desk at the far end of the room, she saw a man looking at them.

"Oh, excuse me," Pete said, speaking over Maggie's shoulder, "we were looking for the telephone."

"It's there." He gestured toward the table near the sofa, but did not look at Pete. He kept his eyes on Maggie as she came into the library. "You're Miss Walsh, aren't you?" he said after a moment.

"Yes," she replied, surprised he knew her. Nervously she reached up and clutched the top of her robe, pulling it tighter across her chest as Pete went to the phone.

"My name is Grandier," the man said, standing. He took the book he was reading and slipped it into his pocket, and then he came toward her.

"Jacques Grandier?"

"Yes," he answered. "Have we met?"

"Well, no, I don't think so, but you sent me this telegram . . ."

"Really? Why?"

"You don't know about it either?" A wave of disappointment broke inside her. "You offered me the job of redecorating your office complex on Tottenham Court Road."

"But that building is brand new. Why would it need redecorating?"

"I have no idea about that," Maggie answered, angry now at having been misled, "but you cabled me ten thousand dollars, and a first-class air ticket."

"Why, of course," he said, suddenly understanding. "My administrative assistant, Mr. Smyth, must have done it for me. He's often weeks ahead of me on my schedule. We have our fingers into many projects at Grandier Limited. I'm sure Smyth had some other building in mind for you. I'll telephone him later and find out." He kept smiling and asked, "You're here for the weekend, I presume."

"No, we're not house guests. We had a slight accident on the road today, and we're waiting here until our motorbike is repaired."

"Have you met Jason yet?"

"Oh, yes! What a charming man, isn't he?" She glanced at Pete. He was speaking into the telephone.

"Is this Wade's garage? This is Pete Danner— Danner. You know, the smashed-up Triumph? We came in with Mr. Mountolive." He paused to listen.

Maggie moved away from Grandier and walked over to Pete as he said, "Yeah, that's right . . . Anyway, how's the bike?" He shook his head. "Damn it . . . Well, okay. Listen, can you find me a car to rent? See if you can, okay? Call me back at Mountolive's house, would you, please? Thanks a lot."

He hung up the phone and turned to Maggie. "It doesn't look good. They had to order some parts all the way from Ashford. There aren't any car-rental agencies in the village, but he'll call some of the nearby towns and see if they can get us one." Pete stopped and looked at Grandier. "Sorry to have disturbed you, sir."

Grandier shrugged. "No trouble, we are all, as you can see, guests of Jason. I was about to give up my book anyway. It is the cocktail hour—won't you join the rest of us for a drink?"

"Great idea," Pete answered. "Maggie?"

"You go ahead, I've got to go upstairs and change." She smiled nicely at them both, then lingered while they left the library. She wanted the chance to wander through the house. It was such a lovely place, so warm and comfortable. She had felt at home from the moment she crossed the threshold.

She went to the top of the stairs, then turned left, away from her bedroom, and into the Portrait Hall. The hall was lit by windows and a high skylight, but outside it was already dusk and growing dark. Maggie walked slowly past the dozens of old family portraits until, near the opposite end of the hall, she spotted a painting of Mountolive himself.

Unlike his ancestors, who stood stiff and formal, he was posed in an armchair with his legs crossed and his hands folded in his lap, a slight smile on his lips.

Beyond the last portrait there was a door built into the wood paneling. Maggie turned the knob and pushed, swinging it open. Through the doorway, she could see another landing and a second staircase, leading, it appeared, to a third floor.

"How big *is* this place?" she whispered out loud, and stepped through only to confront Adams. The nurse's white uniform flashed in the dim light of the stairwell.

Maggie jerked back and gasped, "Oh, God, you scared me! I didn't think anyone was here." She leaned against the door frame, trembling.

"May I help you, Miss Walsh?" Adams asked coldly. "I trust Mr. Danner is well?" She had hold of the door and was moving Maggie back, out of the stairwell and into the Portrait Hall.

"Oh...yes, he is..." Maggie said. "I was just looking around." She smiled apologetically as Adams closed the door behind her, and they moved into the middle of the hall. "The Mountolives must have lived here for hundreds of years," Maggie added, changing the subject and nodding toward the long rows of portraits.

Adams glanced at the paintings and then said quietly, "Yes. They have a long history of survival at Ravenshurst."

"Are all of these Mr. Mountolive's relatives?" Maggie asked, looking around.

"Well, yes, this gentleman here was one of his cousins. He served in the Sudan with Winston Churchill." She crossed the narrow hall to point out another ancestor, saying, "These older portraits are mostly from Mr. Mountolive's mother's side."

"It is an old family, then?"

"Oh, yes, quite." Adams glanced at Maggie, as if trying to determine what more to tell her, then continued, "The family originated in Norfolk as far back as the thirteenth century. They settled in Kent in 1424, this man here, Sir Thomas." She paused in front of the portrait of a very young man. The painting was old and had been damaged by time. The face was barely visible beneath the layers of varnish. Then Adams moved along the hallway, pointing out more Mountolives. "This is Sir James. He was sheriff of Kent in 1497, and it was he who actually purchased this property."

"How big is Ravenshurst?"

"Quite big," Adams answered, but did not provide any more details.

"Does Mr. Mountolive do anything? I mean, does he work?" Maggie was not sure what questions were acceptable. The nurse's curtness had unsettled her.

Adams frowned. "Ravenshurst is his work, Miss Walsh."

"Yes, I know, but does he have a . . . career?"

"Career? Oh, yes, but not in the way you Americans think of it. The Mountolive family have always been farmers, except, of course, for serving in the British army. This man, Sir Edmund, was knighted in battle in 1513, and later appointed the lieutenant in charge of the Tower of London. But, no, the men have not had *careers*."

"Has Mr. Mountolive been knighted?"

Adams slowly shook her head. She was standing

again in front of the portrait of Jason. "No," she answered slowly, "I am afraid the English peerage is too jealous of his wealth and power to bestow more honors on Mr. Mountolive."

"It is a wonderful painting of him, isn't it?" Maggie spoke up, trying to say something nice.

"Yes. Mr. Mountolive was a very striking person."

Maggie glanced at her. "You make him sound like an old man," she said, smiling slightly.

Adams turned away from the portrait and slowly the women left the room, pausing again at the second-floor hallway. "We will be serving drinks soon," she stated. "Do come as soon as you are ready." And then she went down the stairs to the first floor.

"Thank you." Maggie stood a moment longer watching the nurse descend the steps, then went on to her own room and never once looked up, never once saw the man standing in the shadows of the third floor.

———

Chapter Eleven

"Is that her?" Karl whispered to Jacques, looking up from their backgammon game. Maggie was standing in the minstrel gallery above the Grand Hall, looking down at them, and at Barbara Kirstenburg playing the piano.

"You should concentrate on the game, Karl, or you're going to lose," Jacques answered, not taking his eyes off the board.

"I never lose, my friend," Karl answered curtly.

"Nor do I, my friend." Jacques caught the German's eyes and held them while he shook the dice.

"Someone always does."

"Someone must, yes, but never me." He tossed the dice.

Karl grinned, leaning away from the table and momentarily relaxed, breaking the sudden tension that had developed between them. Usually their games were friendly matches, but tonight was different.

"Which of us *will* lose?" Karl asked curiously. As he spoke, he noticed Pete walk hesitantly into the room and look around.

"Perhaps only him." Jacques too had seen the American, and he raised his eyebrows, indicating the young man.

Before Karl could reply, Barbara called out to Pete.

"I know you!" She raised her glass, nodded to him and sipped the champagne.

Pete smiled, thankful that someone had made it easier for him to enter the roomful of strangers.

"I don't think so," he replied, stepping closer to the piano.

"Oh, yes, I've seen you before—but you look different with clothes on." She paused to sip her drink. "You were showing yourself at an upstairs window."

"Showing myself?" Pete frowned, then grinned self-consciously. "Oh, I understand, you came in on the chopper—helicopter—this afternoon."

"You should be ashamed of yourself. Now go mix yourself a drink." She nodded toward the bar.

"Where's the other lady that came with you?"

"Maria? She should be in her pool." Barbara returned to the keyboard, watching the sheet music as she played.

"*Her* pool?" Pete paused, a bottle of Chivas Regal in his hand.

"Jason is a very generous man," Karl called from the backgammon table.

"Particularly where Maria is concerned," Barbara remarked offhandedly, fingers moving deliberately over the keys.

"She must be some swimmer to have a pool built just for her."

"Oh, yes, she is quite a swimmer," Karl said, laughing.

"Indeed," Barbara added. "Back in Rome she has her office in a swimming pool. Now, young man, please fetch me another glass of champagne. I don't wish to spend this cocktail hour talking about Maria Gabrielli." She waved him away.

"Young man?" Karl turned in his straight-back chair. "Where is your friend, Miss Walsh?"

"Oh, she's coming. I left her trying to decide what to wear. We haven't much in the way of formal clothes in our saddlebags."

One brief look at the other guests as they crossed the lawn had told Maggie that it would be impossible for her to dress properly for dinner. The best she could find was a clean pair of slacks and a white silk shirt that she hoped everyone would recognize as expensive.

She put the shirt on, then combed out her hair and let it hang loose. She knew it made her look unsophisticated, but that, if nothing else, might serve as her excuse: maybe they'd think she was too young to know what to wear at dinner. She dressed at her leisure to give Pete a chance to meet everyone in the Grand Hall. By the time she made an appearance, he would have charmed them all.

She had come halfway down the stairs when the heavy front doors flew open, and the houseman came inside loaded down with luggage. Behind him was a dark, curly-haired young man, even younger than Maggie. He was dressed in boots, jeans and a wolfskin overcoat that he loosened as he strode through the door.

"Where is everyone?" he said loudly in a British accent. "Did they get here yet, Harry?"

"Oh, yes, sir. They're having cocktails." Harry set the luggage down and reached for the man's coat. "Shall I take your things, sir?"

The man spun around to give Harry his heavy long coat and spotted Maggie on the stairs.

"Hey, now!" He grinned immediately, pleased at the sight of her. "Don't tell me. You're Maggie. Maggie...Maggie..." He snapped his fingers. "Maggie Walsh!" He moved toward the staircase to shake her hand. "All the way from old L.A. Hi. I'm Clive. Just arrived myself from the U.S. of A."

"Hello," Maggie said quietly, shaking hands, then nodded toward the Grand Hall. "I was just getting my courage up to come down and meet everyone."

"Well, come on, then. You get my courage up and I'll get your courage up. Harry told me about your accident. You okay now?" He looked concerned.

"Oh, sure. Mr. Mountolive picked us right out of the hedge."

Clive stared curiously at her, then burst out

laughing, saying, "Did he, now? Yeah, I bet he did, too."

Behind them, Harry moved up the stairs, saying, "I'll put your luggage in your usual room, sir."

"You do that, mate. Christ, I need a drink. Come on, Mag, come and meet the rest of the pack."

He slipped her arm in his and they moved toward the Grand Hall, Clive whispering as they walked. "I'm the same way, myself, when I come to Ravenshurst."

"Do you come often?"

"Only when Jason calls," he said, and pushed open the door, sweeping her into the room with him. "Dah! Dah! And now, folks—for my next guest, Miss Maggie Walsh!" He spun her out before him like a dance partner, Maggie laughing at his routine.

Karl was the first to reach her. "Well, well, well . . . The six united at last."

"Yes?" She smiled at the old man politely, waiting for him to explain, but he was already looking at her companion.

"Good evening, Clive." Karl shook his hand.

"Hi, Karl . . . Hi, everybody." He leaned closer to Maggie and whispered, "See? They're okay, really. Almost human."

"Stop it, Clive!" She turned away laughing, as Pete came over.

"Hi, sweetie." He kissed her softly on the cheek, as if to show everyone who Maggie belonged to, then looked at Clive and extended his hand, saying, "I'm Pete Danner, nice to meet you."

Clive seemed momentarily startled at Pete's presence, then recovered quickly. "Nice to meet you, chap. Always room for one more Yank."

"And where's Mr. Mountolive?" Maggie asked, looking at the other guests.

"He's resting. I'm sure we'll see him later," Karl explained. He moved closer to Maggie and added in a low voice, "Actually, Miss Walsh, I am very glad to meet you."

"That's very nice, sir." She moved away, as if to make herself a drink, but he followed and continued: "We have all been looking forward to this very much."

"Oh, you have? That's nice." She frowned. What in the world was he talking about?, she wondered.

"Can I mix you up a lovely one, Maggie?" Clive asked, approaching her on the other side, "or are you like our Miss Kirstenburg who insists on chilled glasses of Roederer Cristal '61."

"I think a glass of champagne would be wonderful," she answered, joining forces with the other woman, "and what about Pete? Does he have a drink?" She looked around, spotting him just as he set down his glass and called out into the hall, "Hey, Harry! About tomorrow ... Wait a sec, will ya? ..."

There was no answer from the hall. Pete took off after the houseman, but when he stepped into the foyer, Harry had disappeared. One of the doors off the hall was open and he walked over and glanced inside. It was the entrance to the pool. He followed the passageway to the second-floor balcony and looked down at the water.

Maria was backstroking leisurely across the length of the pool, her arms and legs barely causing a ripple. She looked up at Pete on the balcony, and asked smilingly, "Coming in?", the sound of her voice carrying across the water.

"They said you could swim," Pete called to her. His voice at first was too loud, and he softened it, adding, "No wonder Mountolive built this for you."

"Grazie." She smiled nicely at his compliment.

"Did you see anyone come in here?" he asked, looking down at the small terrace below the balcony.

"No." She shook her head, then touched the edge of the pool, flipped over and smoothly pulled herself out, sitting on the edge and letting her feet dangle in the water.

"Soon it is dinner, no?" she asked, drying her short blonde hair with a towel.

"Not yet." Pete motioned toward the water. "Swim some more," he asked, as if he were enjoying the performance.

Pleased with the unexpected audience, she jumped up and stepped out on the low board at the other side of the pool. She walked to the end of the board, turned her back and edged her heels to the tip. She raised her arms straight over her head, stretched up on tiptoes and paused, concentrating on the jump.

She was quite beautiful, Pete thought. The kind of long, thin body that he liked.

"Busy?" Maggie asked, sliding up next to him as he leaned over the banister.

"Oh, no, I was just, you know, hanging out here, killing some time until dinner."

"See anyone interesting?"

"Interesting? No, I don't think so."

"Did you find Harry?"

"Harry? Harry who?" He wouldn't take his eyes off Maria.

Maggie dug her elbow into his side, with enough force so it hurt. "She's got a better body than I do, doesn't she?" she said wistfully, knowing it was true.

Pete wrapped his arm around her and hugged her closer, looking away from Maria. "Yes," he whispered, "but it's you that I love." He touched her lips with his.

They heard the diving board bounce once more and looked up as Maria gracefully did a flip, knifing into the water without a splash. Pete waited until she surfaced before he applauded.

"Isn't she fantastic!" he said.

"Yes, but not very nice. I met her earlier when I went to get the bandages. She seemed very jealous of Jason Mountolive, told me in so many words not to put the make on him, that Jason was all hers. I'm not interested in Jason, and besides I've got you. That's more than she can say." She linked her arm in his and whispered, "Hey, buddy, when's bedtime?"

"Just as soon as dinner's over. Let's see if we can hurry them along." Pete stood up and waved at Maria. "See you at dinner," he called.

Maria waved back, and as they left the balcony she began to swim the length of the pool, doing two laps of the backstroke, then the breaststroke, then the crawl. She swam hard, without a break, and she never saw the small white cat when it slipped through the door and ran silently down from the balcony to sit at the edge of the pool, watching her do her laps.

After half a dozen turns, Maria pulled up at the

deep end and rested. One more lap, she thought, and then she'd have to change for dinner. This time, she decided, she'd swim the entire length of the pool underwater.

The white cat ran to her swiftly and slid up against her, arching its back against her head. Maria jerked away and slipped into the water. "Scat," she yelled, and splashed water at the animal. She hated cats; they were sneaky and dangerous, and she half believed the old Italian folk legend that they sucked the breath from babies. The cat jumped away from the splash of cold water, hissing at the attack and flashing its teeth. Then it stood passively as Maria took a deep breath and kicked away from the side, diving toward the bottom of the pool.

She swam slowly and steadily until she reached the wall of the shallow end. Then, moving gracefully, hardly stirring the water, she started back toward the deep end. She loved the silence at the bottom of the pool, the look of the deep green water. The water was safe and comforting; sometimes she wished she had been born an amphibian.

When she was almost at the other end, she kicked and let herself climb slowly to the surface. She could see the bottom of the diving board shimmering above her. Perhaps she would take one last dive before she left the pool, she thought. Thank God for Jason's gift; it was the only thing that made the meetings at Ravenshurst possible. And thank God, she thought also, for Jason, who had made everything possible for her, and then her body slammed hard into the surface of the water, plunging her down again. In the shock, she almost lost what little breath she had, but she kicked again and rose swiftly to the surface only to slam again into the surface of the water.

Oh, my God! she panicked. What is it? She dropped down and swam several yards farther before she came up, but again her body struck the surface. She could not break through the water and into the air.

Her lungs hurt. The ribs squeezed against her diaphragm and crushed her chest. She gasped and a gulp of water filled her mouth.

"Oh, God, I'll drown!" her mind screamed, and she banged wildly at the surface. The blows echoed through the two-story pool room.

The white cat ran down the pool and onto the diving board. It sat watching as Maria struggled beneath the water, watching with the same intense interest with which it would follow a goldfish in a bowl. It even raised its leg and pawed the air, as if to catch the floating image.

Maria could not see the cat. She was pressed against the surface of the water, her beautiful face distorted as she tried to breathe any air that might possibly be trapped under the shield. But there was no air and the water would not let her go.

She clung to the slippery, invisible shield until her lovely body filled with water and she suffocated. The last thing she saw was someone on the balcony, leaning over the railing and watching her die. The figure was distorted, a shape shimmering through the water. It looked like Jacques Grandier, she thought, and then again it could have been Jason when he was a younger man. She did not know. She did not now really care.

She was only tired, and her body sank lazily to the bottom, her long arms and legs limp and useless as she turned and sank. Her body hit the bottom in slow motion, the arms and legs askew, twisted like a doll's broken limbs. Her mouth hung open and gasping. She stared wild-eyed around the pool as her body turned, her eyes open and shocked, as if she had just recognized a terrible truth.

Then, ever so slowly, her body rose to the surface, tumbling gracefully, picking up speed as it neared the top and finally popped onto the surface like a cork, floating there face down in the center of the still water, her eyes staring intensely at the Ravenshurst crest imprinted on the bottom of the pool.

The cat at the end of the diving board watched the motionless body a little longer, then grew bored, yawned, and trotted off silently, slipping out through the balcony to join the other weekend guests of Jason Mountolive.

Chapter Twelve

"Ah! There you are!" Jacques said, coming into the Grand Hall. "I was wondering where you had gone." He walked to where she sat, alone on the sofa.

"I was watching Maria swim." She answered politely, glancing up from the art book, but not giving him any reason to join her. She did not like Jacques, or any of the others, she had decided, except Clive, who was silly but cute. She sipped her champagne and looked around for Pete, who was standing by the piano. Just the sight of him calmed her. She did not know why, but she always felt better when he was near her.

"You know, I think you and I should join forces," Jacques said quietly, sitting very close to her on the sofa.

"According to Mr. Smyth, we already have," Maggie replied, tossing her head back to clear her hair from her face. She didn't mind being rude to him. His smooth, easy phoniness offended her.

"Yes, well, I rang up Smyth about you and, as I suspected, we need your talents for a project much more challenging than the London office."

"Such as?" she asked directly. She decided immediately that if he did offer her another job, she would insist he double her $10,000 fee.

"Such as luxury hotels on the Mediterranean," Barbara interrupted, moving away from Karl and Pete to join their conversation.

"Not necessarily," Jacques protested. "I don't own them *all*." He glared at Barbara, angry that she was interrupting his private conversation.

"But you own all the people who own them, darling," Barbara retorted. There was nothing nice about her voice.

God, what a bunch of creeps, Maggie thought.

"What do the rest of you do, anyway?" Maggie asked, raising her voice and attracting everyone's attention.

"Karl here was decorated by Hitler three days before the bunker fell," Clive said quickly, speaking from behind the pages of a magazine. He then pulled himself up from his slouch and added, "He now makes weapons in Germany that he hustles in every poor country of the world. Karl's idea of fun is to go out in the back of beyond, some place like Ethiopia, where he's just been—" Clive nodded toward Karl, showing him he did know—"and sell guns and tanks and missiles to *both* sides. He lives, however, in constant fear that all the tribes in Africa will someday wise up and stop killing each other off."

"Oh, Clive," Karl said humorously, moving into the center of the room to break Clive's eye contact with Maggie, "you English have never forgiven me for losing the war but winning the peace."

"Now there's Barbara," Clive continued, his voice louder and more insistent. He had a lot to say and he wanted Maggie to hear him. "Barbara's family in Latvia couldn't give her much of a debut, but with a little help from her 'friend,' she now has one of the leading houses of haute couture in Paris. And have you met our other little sweetheart, Maria Gabrielli?" He paused and looked at Maggie.

"Maria, the swimmer?"

"Yes, lovely Maria. Well, she started out in the romantic slums of Naples and ended up the most prominent . . . hostess in Rome."

"Well, you all appear to be very successful," Maggie said, trying to keep the peace. She had not realized that Clive was so hostile toward the others.

"Not everyone," Karl answered coolly, lighting a cigarette. "Clive always wanted to be an English gentleman, and look at him now."

"What do you do, Clive?" Maggie interposed quickly.

"I'm in the music business, luv."

"In Europe, Miss Walsh," Jacques murmured, "our friend Clive Jackson *is* the music business."

"If you can call that noise music," Barbara interjected. She moved away from the group, but stopped before the mirror and looked up at herself, concealing her attention to her appearance by adjusting an earring.

"Well, where does Mr. Mountolive fit in?" Maggie asked. She glanced at all of them, but no one replied until Jacques leaned closer and asked quietly, "How much have you been told?"

"Told? What do you mean?...Nothing." She looked around at the roomful of strangers. "What are you getting at?"

"We five owe everything to Jason Mountolive," Jacques answered. "Everything. When he calls us, we come—as you did. I must confess we were not expecting your young man, but with you ... well, we make six. Does that mean anything to you? The Six?"

She slowly shook her head. "I haven't the foggiest idea what you're talking about. The six what?" She looked around at all of them, but they said nothing, only continued to stare at her.

"Didn't Jason explain?" Jacques asked slowly.

Maggie shook her head impatiently.

"But why are you here?" Barbara said.

"We had an accident, Pete and I. Mr. Mountolive was kind enough to help..." Her eyes kept sweeping back and forth across the group, searching their faces for some explanation, but they only stared back at her with expressions of disbelief on their faces.

Then the door burst open and Adams was standing there. "Mr. Grandier," she said, interrupting, "may I speak to you, please?"

"Excuse me, Miss Walsh." Jacques put down his

drink and hurried to the nurse who spoke quietly to him.

"It's Maria," he announced, turning to the group. "Something has happened to her," and then he bolted past Adams, out the door and running toward the pool. Without a word the others rushed after, Karl, then Barbara and Clive.

Maggie looked at Pete.

"What the hell is that all about?" he asked.

"Let's go look!"

From the balcony Maggie and Peter could see Maria floating face down in the pool, her body turning slowly in the slight draft of air from the open door.

"Oh, God!" Maggie whispered. Her hand went to her mouth and she bit into her flesh to keep from crying. The others were at the pool's edge, staring silently. Nobody made a move to pull her out. It was as if they were afraid to touch her body.

Pete ran down the steps and, jerking off his boots, dove into the water. It took him only two strokes to reach Maria, and he pushed her ahead of him to the edge of the pool.

"Help me!" he shouted. "Grab her arms and pull her out."

Clive and Jacques finally reached out and pulled Maria up onto the side of the pool.

Pete hauled himself from the water and, kneeling beside Maria, pressed his mouth against hers and exhaled.

"It's no use, young man," Karl commented. "She's gone."

Ignoring Karl, Pete kept up his mouth-to-mouth

resuscitation, leaning over and pressing his ear against her chest and listening for a heartbeat.

"Young man, please!" Karl said again.

"Shut up, will you?" Pete snapped and began again.

Karl looked at the others and shrugged, then calmly lit another cigarette.

"I'll go and tell Mr. Mountolive," Adams said, "and call the police." She left the pool room, but did not hurry.

"She must have struck her head on the bottom of the pool," Jacques suggested, "or the diving board." He looked toward the group, as if he wanted them to agree with him.

Pete gave up the resuscitation and sat back. He had to take several deep breaths before he could speak. "Then why aren't there any bruises on her head?"

"Oh, she probably just drowned," Barbara tossed off impatiently. Jacques nodded quickly, agreeing.

"Accomplished swimmers don't just drown," Pete answered, not looking at her.

"Well, there isn't anything any of us can do now," Karl added. He had already moved away from the body.

"She might have been saved if one of you had moved a little bit faster." Pete raised his voice accusingly.

"It doesn't take long to die, young man," Karl remarked. He snapped open his gold lighter and lit another cigarette, watching Pete while he did. His eyes were small and bright blue. A cold son of a bitch, Pete thought, then said to the group: "If you'll excuse me, I'm going to have to change into some dry clothes." He looked at Maggie and nodded, indicating he wanted her to come with him. "When the police come, we'll be in our room." He took Maggie by the hand and they went upstairs to the balcony. At the top of the stairs, he glanced back; they were looking up, watching them leave.

"That's some bunch," Pete whispered. "They don't even care that Maria is dead."

"They weren't even helping her," Maggie said as they went up the staircase. "She was just floating in the middle of the pool and no one would get her out. Even that nurse didn't try to revive her; she came and told Jacques without even bothering to make sure Maria was dead. I'm going to tell Mountolive."

"Forget it, Maggie. Maria's dead; it won't do her any good. Let the police ask Adams why she didn't try to rescue her."

They had reached the second floor and went toward their room, still whispering, as if afraid to be overheard.

"Why is there a nurse here anyway?" Maggie asked, opening the door of their room. "Isn't that a bit odd?"

"Maybe she isn't really a nurse. That could be why she wouldn't go near Maria."

Pete closed the door behind him and said out loud, safe within the privacy of the bedroom, "Well, let's make sure he doesn't do us any favors. I don't know if I could survive them. I nearly killed myself just taking a shower. And now this!" Pete stripped off his wet shirt and paused. "Where is he anyway? We haven't seen him since mid-morning. Some kind of host he's turned out to be."

"He'll be downstairs for dinner," Maggie said, going to the bathroom to get him a towel.

"Well, I won't be. I don't feel like eating."

"Pete, we haven't had anything all day." Maggie handed him the towel and he looped it around her shoulders, pulling her closer. "Don't you want anything?" she asked.

"I want a nice, stiff drink, Scotch preferably, and I want you."

"I think," she whispered, nuzzling close to him and wrapping her arms around his waist, "that it can be arranged."

"Which?"

"Both. Which do you want to start with?"

"The Scotch."

"Okay. I'll be right back." She kissed him on the lips and pulled away.

"Maggie," he said, holding her with the towel a moment longer, "I love you very much."

"And I love you very much, Pete Danner." And then she was gone.

Chapter Thirteen

IN THE GRAND HALL, Maggie stood at the elaborate bar, pouring Pete a double. He was upset about Maria, and the Scotch probably wouldn't help. She wished they had some dope, but they had been afraid to take a chance on carrying anything through English customs. Clive would have grass, she knew, and she made a note to ask him about it later. Then she poured herself a glass of Scotch and went back upstairs. Adams met her on the second-floor landing.

"Oh, Miss Walsh. I was coming to find you." The nurse stood at the top, blocking her way down the hall.

"I was getting us a drink; the accident was very upsetting." As angry as she was with Adams, she found herself apologizing for helping herself to the liquor.

"Miss Walsh, Mr. Mountolive would like to see you now."

"Oh, fine, I'll get Pete." She tried to move by, but Adams blocked her way again, and took the glasses from her. "He wishes to see you only, Miss Walsh." She spoke softly, but there was no question of her purpose. She was not someone who expected to be disobeyed.

"Well, isn't he coming down for dinner?"

"No, I'm afraid not." The nurse did not offer more of an explanation. "It will only take a few minutes. We'll leave the drinks here."

They went through the Portrait Hall, dark now, and past the ancestral portraits, then up the rear staircase to the top floor. It was the older part of the house, Maggie could see, a separate wing that must have predated the main sixteenth-century mansion. The hallway was smaller, darker, and she felt chilled by the dampness of the stone walls.

"The others are here," Adams whispered, stopping at the end of the hall. Then gently she opened the door and stepped back so Maggie could precede her into the bedroom.

The weekend guests of Jason Mountolive glanced up nervously as she entered and then looked away. Maggie could feel the tension in the room.

She looked around the bedroom. It was larger than the other rooms of the house, paneled in the same dark wood. But across the middle of the room was a glass wall that reflected their images back to them. There was no furniture, except six chairs facing the glass partition. To the right was a stainless-steel and black leather nursing station with monitoring equipment.

"What's going on here?" Maggie asked, taking in the elaborate intensive-care equipment.

"Would you all please take your seats?" Adams asked.

"Where's Mr. Mountolive?" Maggie turned toward Adams who now was seated at the nurse's desk. "You said he wanted to see me."

"Margaret... Please make yourself comfortable..." It was Jason Mountolive she heard, but his voice was tired and weak, amplified by a speaker. Maggie spun around, expecting to see him behind her. But there was only her own reflection in the dark glass.

"Jason... Mr. Mountolive," she protested.

The other guests seemed as puzzled as she, but they followed Adams' instructions. As they settled down, facing the glass partition, the nurse lowered the lights in the room. Maggie slid slowly to a seat, strangely enthralled by what was occurring.

As the light dimmed on their side of the glass, it increased dramatically on the other, revealing a brilliantly white-walled room, dominated by an opaque plastic tent. In the center, on the bed, Maggie could see the ghostly outline of a figure.

There was no sound in the bedroom except the heavy rasping of the lung-support equipment, and the EKG needle that scraped across the flowing page. Then they heard Jason's voice, labored and strained, but still powerful, as if almighty.

"Welcome to you all: Clive, Karl, Jacques and

Barbara. I heard of the tragic accident that befell Maria and I join you in your sorrow. I would like to specially welcome Margaret. I have waited many years to meet you."

Maggie sat up on the edge of her chair, shielding her eyes against the intense overhead lights. "Mr. Mountolive?" she asked hesitantly. He sounded like the man she had met hours before, but she wasn't sure. The voice was so old and strained, the voice of a very sick man.

"This meeting is the culmination of my life's work," Jason began again, his voice amplified by the speaker. "You are all shocked, I know, to see how I have failed since we last met. Soon this aging body will be no more, but with your help, I will live on. My legacy is vast, immeasurable. The ring each of you wears is a symbol of power—the power that binds us.... To you, I bequeath my power, my knowledge and my estate. The survivors may divide them equally among yourselves at the moment of my death."

Maggie glanced down the row of chairs at the others. They were all sitting up straight, listening intently, their hands folded in their laps. She noticed for the first time that they all wore silver signet rings, each ring bearing the heavy gothic figure of a bird— the same angry raven that was outlined in mosaic on the bottom of the swimming pool.

"Margaret," Jason summoned, "step forward and receive the blessing of the ring."

She stood slowly. What was happening was like a dream in which she could see that everyone else was crazy—but they treated *her* as if she was the crazy one for not understanding. There was really no rational response to make; she just hoped she could keep talking long enough to get herself out the door.

"Look, Mr. Mountolive, I hope you understand ... I really don't want the ring. I just came to thank you for your hospitality and to say good-bye. Pete is trying to locate a car for us and we'll be leaving later tonight or the first thing in the morning." She turned away from the glass partition and tried to locate the exit in the dark room.

"Please, Margaret," Barbara asked, "go see him." Her hands were shaking.

Maggie tensed, feeling the pressure from the group around her. Perhaps it would be easier to play by their rules, until she could get back to Pete.

She sighed elaborately. "Well, all right." Then she opened the glass door, sliding it silently back, and stepped into the hospital room, moving slowly, carefully, toward the bed. There were metal stands everywhere, plastic tubes and bottles of blood and saline fluid, and more intensive-care equipment— everything that was needed to measure and record all aspects of a patient's circulatory, respiratory, gastrointestinal and renal physiology. They were keeping the man alive, she realized; that was the purpose of all this sophisticated equipment. Now she knew why Nurse Adams was at the mansion. But what she did not understand was how Jason could have been with them that morning, driving around on the back roads of Kent.

Maggie glanced back at the others, but they were hidden in the darkened room and she saw only Adams, stepping forward to slide the glass door closed. Now Maggie was alone with the dying man.

"Where are you?" Jason asked from behind the

plastic curtain, his unamplified voice weaker and more urgent.

Maggie saw the shadowy figure move on the bed.

"Are you near?" Jason asked.

"Yes, I am," Maggie answered quickly, afraid she would upset him and perhaps cause him pain. She stepped between the tubes of fluid and went closer to the head of the bed. She was looking up, making sure she was avoiding the hanging bottles of blood and liquid and so she did not see the crippled hand slip out from between the curtains and reach for her. It was a thin white hand, the skin wrinkled and blotched with cancerous sores, an old, decaying claw with long fingers and yellow nails that curled up like a bird's talons.

Then she saw the hand. It grabbed her by the wrist and held her while its obscene twin slid the ring onto her finger.

At its touch she fainted, fell heavily against the stands of fluid, but Adams was there behind her, to catch Maggie before she could bring harm to Jason Mountolive.

Chapter Fourteen

"I CAN'T GET IT OFF, PETE!" She held her hand under the hot water and rubbed soap under the band. There were tears in her eyes, and she was in pain from struggling with the ring. "Oh, it's awful." She held up her hand again and spread her fingers. The ring was too big for her, too grotesque, the raven's beak open and its claws raised.

"Wait, honey." Pete put his arm around her shoulder. "Don't hurt yourself. When we go to the garage tomorrow, I'll have them cut it off."

Maggie stared at the ring for a moment more. "They're all crazy, Pete," she said.

"That's why we're getting out of here. They're a bunch of wealthy kooks. I'm going downstairs to start scouring Kent for a car. If I have to have them send one from London, then that's what we'll do. I'm getting you away from these people."

"Don't go telephone yet. Stay with me a few minutes, please." She dried her hands, then went inside and crawled into bed, pulling the comforter up over her. Pete tucked it tightly around her body and sat beside her.

"You okay?" he asked. She seemed different since she had come back from Mountolive's room, tense and preoccupied.

"Yes, I think so, but I am tired. It's been a long day, and I'm just scared something else is going to happen."

"Nothing will, I promise."

"Stay with me anyway." Absentmindedly she twisted the ring on her hand, fingering the raven. "What's the purpose of these signet rings, anyway? Mountolive said the ring bound us together. What were they used for?"

"Most titled families in England had them. They became popular in the fifteenth and sixteenth centuries. English gentlemen had their initials and coats of arms put on their crests." He examined the ring closely, holding her hand in his. "This is a rather fine ring, actually."

"I hate it."

"You would have loved it in the sixteenth century. A ring like this meant power and authority."

"I don't care what it meant. I want it off, and I don't want anything more to do with Mountolive. I just want to get away from this house." She took her hand away from Pete and slid it beneath the covers so she could not see the ring.

"But I thought you liked this place. You said it made you feel comfortable."

"Not any more. Not after what they did to me upstairs. God, you should have seen that wrinkled hand. It was horrible."

"It wasn't Mountolive, then?"

She shook her head. "How could it have been? We saw him this morning and he was fine. This was terrible, a diseased hand with long fingernails, hanging skin...God, it gives me the chills every time I think of it grabbing my arm."

"Don't think about it, then." He leaned over and kissed her on each eyelid. "Get some sleep. I'm going downstairs to make those phone calls."

"Don't be too long." She was already drowsy. "And leave the light on," she added, but didn't open her eyes.

Pete sat on the side of the bed a while longer, waiting until he was sure she was asleep, and then he pulled the curtains around the bed. She lay in the dark, her arms clutching a pillow as she breathed deeply. At the door, he flipped off the light. Only the fire lighted the bedroom with an uneven, flickering glow. He stood for a moment to see that everything was in order and then left, closing the door as he did.

In the darkness of the third floor, outside Jason Mountolive's room, Jacques Grandier held the nurse's arm and insisted: "But I have to know! How could he have failed so fast? I saw him only a month ago and he was fine, as healthy as always. And now, my God! I don't even recognize him." He waited for her to answer, to tell him anything, but she merely stared, her face and eyes motionless. She knew, all right. There wasn't anything at Ravenshurst that Adams didn't know.

He could not make her tell him. While Mount-olive lived, Jacques could not threaten her life or her job. There would be changes after he died, though, and Adams would be the first to go. That, Grandier would make certain of.

"Why can't you tell me?" he pleaded. "Look, we've known each other a long time..."

"I have to go." She pulled her arm from his hand and turned, but when he moved toward Mount-olive's room, she paused and said, as if issuing an order, "You won't disturb him, will you...?" Then waited until Jacques walked by her and left the third-floor wing.

In the library, Pete dialed information and listened to a recorded voice say, "All lines are temporarily engaged."

"Goddamn!" He hung up, then tried again immediately.

"Trouble, young man?"

Pete looked up, surprised at not being alone in the library. In the far corner of the room, he saw the white-haired German looking up from a book.

Pete heard the same recorded voice and hung up.

"Having difficulty?" the German asked. Setting aside his book, he stood and came over to Pete, moving slowly on his stiff leg. He stopped near Pete, lit a cigarette, and said once more, "Having difficulty?"

Pete picked up the receiver and tried a third time, hanging up as soon as the recorded announcement began. "I can't get an outside line," he said.

"Yes, that often happens this time of year." He puffed the cigarette slowly, filling his lungs with smoke.

"Everything happens this time of year," Pete replied sarcastically. "I can't get the bike fixed because of missing parts. There are no cars to rent because the tourist season is over. And now I can't get a long-distance telephone line."

"Well, one shouldn't expect the comforts of home..."

"Bullshit! This is Kent, England, not some Third World country." Pete picked up the receiver again and dialed. While he waited, he looked up, idly scanning the paintings on the wall. Karl could tell by the startled expression on his face when his eyes had reached the portrait of the young woman in the dark gown. From that angle she looked remarkably like Maggie, the same large hazel eyes and high cheekbones, the same mouth and fair skin.

"It is uncanny, isn't it?" Karl remarked at his side.

Pete hung up the phone and did not reply.

"Still no luck?"

"I'll try again in the morning." Pete glanced at his watch. "It's too late to do anything now." He was going to say more, to ask Karl about the portrait, but he decided that the less said, the better off they were. If these people wanted to play games and be mysterious about their lives, then why shouldn't he?

"And Miss Walsh?" Karl asked. "Has she retired for the evening?"

"She's upstairs," Pete answered vaguely, then

picked up the phone and tried one final time. He had to get out of this house.

"Would you care for a drink, young man?" Karl asked while he dialed. "A brandy perhaps?"

Pete shook his head and studied Karl. Something was bothering the German. There was a small line of nervous sweat across his upper lip. Then Pete heard the recorded voice and hung up.

"Giving up?" Karl continued to smile, but the smile was forced.

"For the moment." Pete returned the smile, then added, "Well, good night." He started for the door.

"Young man, I wanted..." Karl limped after Pete, determined now to talk.

"Look!" Pete stopped abruptly and pointed his finger at the old man. "My name is Danner, Pete Danner, so would you lay off the 'young man' routine?"

"I'm sorry. Very sorry. I didn't mean to offend you..."

"Forget it." Pete waved the apology aside. It didn't matter. By morning, he'd be done with this crew. He turned and left the room.

Karl Liebknecht stood tensely, his shoulders square and legs apart. He carried the weight of his strong body on his good left leg and it made him look slightly lopsided, like a picture out of line. He did not move for a moment, only quietly kept smoking, taking steady and deep puffs of his cigarette, as he sorted out what he knew.

How could Mountolive deal with that young man? Certainly he wouldn't let Margaret leave after having spent so long trying to find her. Still, how would he be able to keep her? Especially as she had this man to protect her. But Mountolive would find a way; he always had.

Karl stubbed out the cigarette and left the library, going toward the Grand Hall and the drinks. He needed one now, after all the events of the evening. It was Maria's death that upset him most. Just when the Six were finally together, she had to die. And why? It was no accident; he knew Maria Gabrielli did not drown. She was a glutton for life, and her appetite would have kept her from dying in a swimming pool. If not an accident, then who had killed her?

He entered the Grand Hall as Jacques was refilling his glass.

"Good, company," Karl said. "I hate to drink alone."

"I was just thinking of you, Karl," Jacques remarked. He opened the ice bucket and, using the silver tongs, lifted out two cubes.

"Of me?" Karl poured several fingers of brandy into a large snifter.

"Yes, of you, and, of course, the others, especially Margaret." He said her name softly and glanced up at the small balcony to see that no one was there, standing in the shadows.

"Ah, Margaret! Yes, she is on all our minds, I should think." They moved to the sofa and sat down together, close, as if it were mutually understood that they did not wish to speak loudly. "And what do you make of her?" Karl asked, watching the Frenchman over the rim of his globe glass.

"That is difficult to answer. I would like to know

who she is."

"A young woman from America," Karl said, shrugging.

Jacques nodded and smiled wryly. He knew it would be that way, each of them wary of the other. None of them ever knew how much the others had been told. Jason had been very systematic about this, permitting them only parts of the whole puzzle of his legacy.

"It appears to me," Karl offered, "that the woman is here against her will. You saw her upstairs with Jason; she knows absolutely nothing about us."

"Yes, but that was before Maria drowned."

Karl nodded slowly. "And, of course, she has the ring now. That will make a difference. We all have found that to be true."

Jacques nodded again, saying nothing.

He was irritating Karl with his silence and profound looks. Didn't the man understand they were involved in this together, and if one failed, so did the others? Then, before Karl could say more, Jacques responded, said quietly:

"It is possible, you know, that there could be only one, Karl." He watched the German for his reaction and was not surprised to see Karl jump to his feet and sputter: "That's impossible. No one of the Six could inherit it all."

"Have you read *her* book, my friend?" Jack sipped his drink and then added, "I have."

Above, in the minstrels' gallery, Adams waited and watched the men. Their voices were low and difficult to hear, but she heard and understood.

"Where's the book?" Karl demanded, jumping to

his feet. Even from a distance Adams could see his hands trembling and the brandy sloshing in his glass.

"The library." Jacques answered calmly, still sitting on the sofa.

"It's been there all these years?"

"Yes, all these years."

"Well, what does it say?" he demanded.

"It's her life, Karl. Margaret's life."

"But I know her story. We all do; Jason told us."

Jacques laughed shortly, almost contemptuously. "All you think of is the power and the money, Karl. But there is more, much more. Read her book; you will see."

"Why are you telling me so much?" Karl studied the Frenchman, suddenly distrustful. Always, Jacques had been secretive about his own past, and how he had come to know Jason Mountolive. All the others were known by their public scandals, but not Jacques Grandier. His sins were secret, familiar only to Jason himself.

"I tell you," Jacques answered, "because now we need each other. The Six have been assembled, but one has already died." He nodded knowingly and sipped his drink. "If we don't join together, our own fates may be the same as that of Maria Gabrielli."

"You think it was her then, Jacques? Walsh and her young man?"

Grandier shrugged. "I am not sure. You are apprehensive and trembling, but perhaps it was you who killed Maria. After all, as Jason told us, we share equally in his estate, and now we are one less."

"Jacques, you cannot believe that! You think I am an old man, too old for Maria. But years ago, when Jason first found her, we were lovers. I could never have killed her."

"Oh, Karl, save your German sentimentality. We have *all* known Maria; Jason, yes, in his time, and Clive, myself, even Barbara." He raised his eyebrows. "Maria screwed us all because she understood what would happen when Jason died, and she wanted allies. She knew. She had read Margaret's book; I showed it to her myself."

"Knew what?" Karl almost feared to hear the answer.

Jacques paused, waited a moment for Karl to calm himself. "She knew, as we all should, that Jason was her protection, and that her death could only come from one of us. It has been written, Karl. Written by Margaret of Ravenshurst."

Adams stepped out of the gallery into the hallway on the second floor. She did not go directly to Mountolive. There was time, and she did not want to trouble him this late in the evening. It had been a long day and tomorrow would be worse.

She went down the hallway, her rubber-soled shoes silent on the thick carpet. The door of Barbara Kirstenburg's bedroom was open and Adams paused to look in. Barbara was sitting before the vanity table in a silk kimono, rubbing cream into her face. Adams watched quietly until Barbara, sensing someone's presence, looked up and spotted the nurse's reflection in the mirror. Barbara stood and came to face her.

"Good night, Adams," she said coolly and closed the door.

Further along the hall, Adams paused again, this

time at a closed door. She listened a moment for voices, then carefully opened the **bed**room door. The lights were out and the fire had **d**windled. She could see their shadows behind the curtain of the canopy bed. Maggie was closer to Adams, with her back turned toward Pete. She was sleeping, but her rest seemed to be disturbed. She tossed and turned in the bed while Adams stood in the doorway and watched the nightmare occur.

She was inside a house, wandering from room to room. It was empty and dark and she had lost something important, but she did not know what.

And she could hear voices. They were chanting, shouting, and she did not know what they wanted, nor could she find them in the empty house.

She went from room to room, opening doors, endless doors, one after another, and now she was running, trying to get free. She could feel the pain in her chest and she fought to breathe.

Then she was finally out of the house. She stared around in the dark night and saw she had come out on the roof of the huge mansion. She stood high above the ground, among the tall chimneys and the black slate roofing. The voices were blended into an animal roar, and she knew, as all dreamers do, that they were coming for her.

Maggie sat up trembling, trying to catch her breath. She knew she had cried out in the quiet house and it was a moment before she realized it was only a nightmare. She pulled her legs up and leaned her head against her knees.

Pete turned beside her but did not wake up. She

wished he would. She was still trembling with fear, the dream had been so real, so terrifying. She raised her head, pushed her long hair away from her face, and then through the thick curtain she saw someone move by the bedroom door.

"Who is it?" she asked, the fear coming back to her. The figure moved again, silhouetted against the hallway light. Maggie grabbed Pete's shoulder and shook him awake.

"There's someone here," she whispered.

He was out of bed instantly, sweeping the curtains aside and rushing to the door.

There was only the white house cat, sitting crouched in the hallway light. The cat looked up and meowed, then hissed as Pete came closer.

"I'm sorry, Pete." Maggie threw back the blanket and got out of bed. She went to the cat and lifted it into her arms, where it purred and snuggled up. "It wasn't anything," Maggie said, bringing the cat back to bed with her. "I had this terrible nightmare about running through a dark house. I wonder what Freud would make of it."

She settled down again into the pillows, holding the cat to her, and it purred loudly as she gently stroked its back. Pete closed the bedroom door and slipped back in beside her, saying, "Anyone would have nightmares after what you've gone through." He moved to take Maggie in his arms, to comfort her, but the cat hissed and raised its paw, its sharp claws going for Pete's eyes.

"Get that damn cat out of here," he said.

"No, Pete, you just frightened it." Maggie cuddled the cat closer, kissed it lovingly on the forehead. The cat purred again and relaxed.

"No, I didn't. This cat just doesn't like me."

"Let me hold it a little longer," Maggie said, settling down under the heavy blankets. "She makes me feel secure."

"Whatever you want," Pete said curtly. Maggie had turned to the cat and not to him for comfort after her nightmare. But he knew it didn't matter. Tomorrow they would be out of Ravenshurst and he would have her to himself again.

He fell asleep on that reassuring thought while Maggie lay awake slowly stroking the small white cat, comforted by the animal's warmth and its gentle purr of contentment.

Chapter Fifteen

PETE WANTED TO GET away from Ravenshurst early in the morning, before the others were awake. Without disturbing Maggie, he rose, dressed quietly, and packed the saddlebags. Then he went downstairs to find the chauffeur. Adams met him at the bottom of the stairs.

"Would you care for some breakfast, Mr. Danner? We're serving on the side porch; it's rather nice and sunny these days."

"Thank you, but I never eat breakfast."

"Miss Walsh, then? Would she like a good old-fashioned English breakfast?" The nurse smiled. "I could have the maid bring it up to her room, if she preferred."

"No, Miss Walsh is sleeping and I don't want her disturbed. She didn't get much rest last night, thanks to your people's little rituals."

"I beg your pardon." The nurse was frowning. She put on her glasses and peered closely at Pete. The glasses made her eyes bulge.

"Never mind. Where's Harry? I need him to give us a lift into the village."

"I'm afraid that's not possible," Adams answered, in a tone of cool control. "The police have forbidden anyone to leave Ravenshurst."

"The police?"

"They took Signorina Gabrielli's body away early this morning. They particularly wish to speak to you and Miss Walsh, as you were the last ones to see her alive."

"Yeah, well, if they want us, they can find us in town." He walked past her, toward the front door, but she called after him:

"They are coming back to investigate fully. You are legally obliged to stay."

Pete hesitated at the door. Then he turned to say, "Ms. Adams, I've been awake for hours and I didn't hear or see any police this morning. In fact, I don't believe they came out to Ravenshurst, nor do I think you telephoned them last night. But I will tell you what I'm going to do. When I get to the village I'll stop by the police station and tell them that a woman died here last night, and that I think they should investigate the whole lot of you. As for Maggie and myself, we're getting out before anything more happens to us." He pulled open the heavy front door and walked out into the cool March morning.

Adams stood a moment looking after him, watching him stride across the drive, and only then did she allow a smile to creep across her face. Then she turned and went about her business.

Karl and Jacques were up early too, and they stood near the house, loading crossbows. They had set up archery targets far across the lawn and they waved Pete over to join them. But he disregarded the invitation and went to Harry, who had parked the Rolls in the circular drive and was cleaning the windows of the huge car.

"I don't think that young man cares much for us," Karl remarked.

"Nor can we blame him." Jacques smiled as he hooked the front end of the crossbow to a stake, then hauled back the string with both hands and positioned it. The effort of cocking the weapon left him winded and he stopped a moment to regain his breath before shooting. He wondered how Karl, twenty years older than he, could so easily handle the crossbow.

"It's not a question of strength," Karl remarked, watching him. "You need regular practice, my friend, and, I think, more skill. Here, let me show you."

Karl quickly loaded the short bolt and positioned himself. Fitting the gun's stock firmly against his leather shoulder patch, he set the sights and pulled the trigger. The arrow flew over the forty yards of grass and thumped into the target.

Pete could hear the arrow hit from where he stood near the Rolls, and he glanced up to see that Karl had scored a bulls-eye. Then he asked the chauffeur, "Harry, we'd like to go into the village this morning. Would you drive us?"

"Very good, sir, whenever you're ready." The chauffeur continued wiping the front windshield.

"How about now?"

"Very good, sir." Harry folded away his cleaning rag and opened the rear door of the Rolls.

"Well, I'll have to get Miss Walsh and our luggage." Pete backed off. He had expected the driver to protest, to make some excuse.

"Very good, sir," Harry nodded.

His sudden friendliness was encouraging. Pete relaxed and said, "Hey, Harry, level with me. What's really wrong with Mountolive?"

Harry straightened up and glanced around before he said in a whisper, "Mr. Mountolive is ill, sir."

"He didn't look sick yesterday. He looked to me like he was in great shape. What gives?"

Harry paused a moment and then added, "Actually, Mr. Mountolive is dying, sir." The chauffeur looked down as he replied, and bit his lower lip.

"I'm sorry to hear that. I had no idea . . ."

Harry nodded. "It's hitting the staff rather hard, sir. We've been in Mr. Mountolive's service for a good many years."

"What will happen to you, Harry? To all of you at Ravenshurst?"

"Oh, we'll be taken care of, sir. The new master of Ravenshurst will see to that."

"And who's that?" Pete was curious now. He had listened to Maggie's bizarre story of what had happened in Mountolive's bedroom and couldn't believe that any of it was true: that Mountolive was dying, or that he was going to turn over his estate to these people, one of whom was Maggie.

"It will go to his heirs, sir," Harry replied uneasily.

"What heirs?" Pete pressed. "Who exactly?"

"Well, I wouldn't know, sir." Harry tried to edge away. "Mr. Grandier and Mr. Liebknecht would have a better idea, sir. Perhaps you should ask one of those gentlemen." He nodded toward Jacques and Karl who were reloading their crossbows.

"Our young friend seems very inquisitive," Karl said softly. "Harry knows better than to say too much, doesn't he?"

"Oh, yes, we needn't worry about Jason's staff. Adams keeps them well in line, and, of course, their future depends on this weekend." He glanced across the lawn at Harry and Pete standing together. Pete did make him nervous. He wondered why the young man was spending so much time talking to Mountolive's chauffeur.

"All of our futures depend on this weekend," Karl remarked, that slight, ironic smile forming on his lips. "I just wish we didn't also have to contend with them." Karl nodded toward Pete. "It would make the outcome of this weekend, how would you say in English, less complicated?" He hooked the crossbow on the stake and jerked back the string.

"Perhaps we won't need to," Jacques replied. "I believe our young friends are leaving us." It would be too much to hope for, Jacques knew, that she would walk away from the fortune of Ravenshurst. But perhaps she didn't understand, didn't recognize what waited for her.

Or maybe it was only the young man who was leaving. He had to find out. "Excuse me a moment," he said, setting his loaded crossbow down on the iron bench.

Karl watched Jacques walk toward the Rolls, wondering what the Frenchman had in mind. He knew Jacques wouldn't try to stop the young man; they all secretly wanted the Americans out of Ravenshurst. Karl looked past Jacques. Pete was still talking to Harry, standing by the open door of the Rolls. There were only the two of them in the driveway.

Karl raised his crossbow and aimed, taking into consideration the wind and the distance, and concentrating on his target. He did not notice the white cat run across the lawn and rush up to the crossbow on the bench, nor see the cat sniff the crossbow and lick at the trigger.

Karl squeezed the trigger of his crossbow and the bolt ripped loose, sped through the silent morning. An arrow flew past Jacques, missing him by inches, and should have hit Pete except that he had abruptly stepped away from the Rolls. The arrow pierced the inlaid wood of the car door, only inches from his head.

After a split second of shock, Pete dove behind the car. The chauffeur threw himself into the back seat. "Blimey, sir, that was close!" he said, a few seconds later.

Pete picked himself up off the gravel and saw the two men. Jacques had stopped at the edge of the drive and was looking back at Karl, who was now running toward them.

"Which one of you clowns—?" Pete shouted, coming out from behind the car.

Karl called out, "Are you all right?"

"Only because you're such a lousy shot."

"Please forgive me," Jacques spoke up, realizing immediately what had happened. "I left the crossbow loaded...and the cat..." He was trembling, realizing how close the arrow had come to hitting him. Jacques stood straight and asked Pete formally, "Would you accept my profound apology?"

Angry and still trembling from the close call, Pete looked at both of them. He was running out of good fortune, he thought. First the car, then the hotwater knob, and now a misfired crossbar. The accidents were too close, too coincidental. He had to get away from Ravenshurst before someone got lucky.

"We'll meet you here in front of the house, Harry," Pete said, ignoring Jacques.

"Very good, sir." The chauffeur went around to the driver's seat.

Inside the house, Adams was waiting for him at the bottom of the staircase. Before she could object again to their leaving, he cut her off. "You can tell Mountolive that we're leaving Ravenshurst before his hospitality kills us both." Then he brushed past her and took the steps two at a time.

Maggie was out of bed and dressed. She was pulling on her boots as he rushed into the room. "I'm ready," she said, standing.

"Good! I've got Harry waiting for us downstairs. Let's get the hell out of this place. They almost killed me just now with their morning archery."

Karl moved closer to Jacques and whispered, "They're leaving. Do you think that's possible?

Won't Jason object?"

"How can he? Jason is upstairs, dying."

Karl felt immediately better, thinking of that possibility. "If she goes, that's one less to share the legacy, Jacques," he said.

Instead of answering, Jacques looked toward the house. He could see Adams watching from the windows of the Grand Hall. He nodded, but she turned away without acknowledging him.

"Perhaps Harry won't drive the Americans into the village," he said softly.

"Of course he will! I heard him say so." The German was worried again. "I'll go make sure."

Karl moved around to the driver's seat as Harry turned on the engine. The Rolls purred smoothly.

"Harry, you're taking them into the village, correct?" Karl asked.

The chauffeur did not answer but shifted the Rolls into first.

"Wait! They're coming." He put his hand on Harry's shoulder, but the chauffeur did not stop. The car moved along the driveway.

Pete was coming out of the house when he saw the Rolls drive off. Dropping the saddlebags he sprinted across the lawn, trying to cut the car off. He reached the Rolls and banged on the door, shouted to Harry, but the chauffeur jammed the pedal to the floor and the heavy car spun away, tearing up gravel and roaring out of reach.

"That son of a bitch!" Pete swore. He couldn't catch him. The car had already disappeared into the woods below the house. He stood for a moment to catch his breath, and then went back to Maggie and the two men. "You're a real pain in the ass," he shouted to Karl. "Why the hell did you send him away?"

"But I didn't. I told him to wait. . . . I'm terribly sorry, young man."

"The hell you are! And I told you, the name is Danner. Pete Danner."

"Pete," Maggie whispered, touching his arm. "Forget it."

"Forgive me, Mr. Danner. I didn't mean to offend you." Karl extended his hand. "Would you accept my apologies?"

Pete glanced at Karl's outstretched hand, but did not shake it. Instead he turned to Maggie and said, "Come on, let's take a walk."

When they were out of hearing, Maggie said, "Pete, I think you're taking this too seriously. Harry will drive us into town later, that's all. Adams probably gave him an errand to do for Jason."

"There's no way this gang of clowns is going to keep me here an hour longer," he said grimly. "We'll walk out of this place if we have to."

They passed the gardener, who had started a small rubbish fire, and walked toward the barns. The stables were behind the mansion, separated from the main house by a cobblestone yard.

The stable boy had saddled the chestnut mare and tied her to a post while he walked around to the front of the house. Passing them on the way, he smiled and tipped his cap to Maggie, his heavy boots slapping the wet cobblestones as he walked.

Pete looked at the saddled horse, then checked to see if the stable boy had disappeared. "Care for a morning ride, milady?" he said.

She grinned. "I think that's a wonderful idea."

They walked nonchalantly through the archway and into the stable yard, looking for more Ravenshurst staff, but the yard was empty.

"The tack room," Pete said, pointing it out for Maggie, and ran the other way himself, toward the horses.

In the tack room, Maggie picked up the first saddle, bridle and blanket she could find and stepped outside again, keeping close to the stable wall. Pete had gone into the loose-box and brought out a second horse.

"Where is he?" Pete asked, taking the horse blanket from her.

Maggie looked between the horses. "He stopped to talk to the gardener. His back is to us."

Pete slid the blanket onto the horse, then took the light English saddle from Maggie and threw it across the horse's back, moving carefully so as not to frighten the animal.

"I'll take this one. You ride the chestnut," Pete instructed, and bent down to pull the girth strap under the horse. "Get up!"

Maggie slipped the reins off the ring and pushed the chestnut away from the wall, to give herself room to mount.

"Hey! Where you going?" the stable boy shouted, as Maggie swung her leg over the chestnut.

"Go ahead, Mag," Pete cried and she kicked the big chestnut in the flanks; the horse bolted forward and headed for the archway.

The stable boy let her go and went for Pete, grabbing him from behind. Pete reacted immediately, jamming his elbow into the man's stomach and pushing him off his back. He turned to finish him off. The man was stronger than Pete, and bigger, and when he scrambled up from the cobblestones, he grabbed the handle of a pitchfork.

Pete kicked out before the man could regain his balance, clipping his chin and sending him reeling back. Then Pete jerked the strap tight and swung up on the horse, which was skittish now and frightened by the violence. It bucked and reared and almost threw him, but he yanked the horse under control and raced it toward the archway.

"Geoff! Stop 'em!" the stable boy shouted to the gardener at the archway.

The old man dipped his straw broom into the rubbish fire and turned it on Pete as the horse raced past. Pete kicked out at the gardener as he passed, knocking the flaming broom from the old man's hands. Then he leaned down, his head tucked close to the horse's neck, and they raced through the archway and into the fields.

Maggie had turned away from the driveway; it would be harder to follow them, she realized, if they stayed in the fields and woods. She glanced back and saw Pete approaching, then looked ahead and set herself on the horse as they approached a low hedge. The chestnut took it in a smooth jump.

Pete reached her side and shouted, "Okay?"

She nodded, then indicated the wooden rail fence before them, and they pulled the horses apart and made the jump. They galloped side by side across another clear field, keeping away from the flocks of sheep and herds of cattle, riding fast and not caring in what direction they were headed. They only wanted to put distance between them and Ravenshurst.

Maggie felt wonderful, out of the gloomy house and free of them all. She glanced over at Pete and saw him smile, and she grinned back. It was okay now, she realized. Everything was all right.

They kept the horses racing for over a mile, cutting across pasture land, until they crested a small, smooth knob of a hill and drew the exhausted animals to a stop. Less than a mile away they could see a church steeple and the red tile roofs of a village.

"Is that it?" Pete asked, panting and out of breath.

"I'm not sure. My sense of direction is all screwed up." Maggie stood up in the stirrups and searched the horizon. She could see Ravenshurst way behind them, a small house from that distance. There were other farms and estates, glimpses of roofs and barns, but nothing that was large enough for a village. "It must be," she finally said.

"There's a church, anyway," Pete answered, urging his horse forward, "and we can get some help . . . call the police."

"The police? Why?"

"To find out if Adams really did call the cops. I don't believe her. And I want to find out about this Mountolive. I don't buy this bullshit about his dying. That's all part of the charade."

They walked the horses down the hill, found a gate in the stone wall, and picked up again into a trot as they rode in the middle of the narrow tarmac road. The road twisted and turned and followed the contour of the land toward the village. More houses were visible through the buffer of trees, and Maggie saw that they were approaching the same small town where they had left the bike. They were within a half mile of the village when they heard the truck.

Pete glanced around and saw it racing toward them. "Let's go, Mag!" He dug his heels into the horse's flanks and whipped it into a gallop again.

They kept to the center of the road, but could not outdistance the truck. Pete glanced around and saw the truck had closed the gap between them to less than a hundred yards. There was no escape, no room on either side of the road in which to pull off and let the truck pass. The stone walls were flush against the tarmac.

Ahead Pete spotted a cattle-crossing sign. There would be space there, he knew, a break in the wall, and he yelled at Maggie to pull off, but she couldn't hear him over the horse's hoofs and the roar of the diesel engine.

He moved his horse closer, shouted and pointed to the cattle crossing. She nodded, slowed the chestnut enough to rein it into the small space. The truck roared past her, still behind Pete.

His horse had slowed, exhausted from the morning gallop, and the truck was pressing, pinning them against the stone wall. He was afraid the horse would buck and throw him into the curve, crush him against the stone wall. He pulled hard, tried to stop the horse, but the animal was out of control. It raced the massive truck, heading blindly toward the stone impasse of the curve coming up.

Then, unexpectedly, the truck sped ahead, outraced him, reached the turn and skidded through the close corner and out of sight. Pete gradually slowed his horse, which was trembling still with fright, its body lathered with sweat on the cold morning.

"That crazy bastard!" Pete said, still struggling with his nervous animal as Maggie caught up.

"Whoever it was, he wasn't after you, Pete," Maggie said. "It was me he wanted to kill. Once I got off the road safely, he drove right past you. He could have run you up against the wall, but he didn't. He was just trying to kill me." She looked toward the village. The road ahead was still empty.

"Well, I'm not giving whoever it was another chance," Pete said. "Let's get out of here." He pulled the horse around and raced the final half-mile into the quiet English village.

Chapter Sixteen

THE STREETS WERE STILL EMPTY, as they had been the day before.

"Where is everyone?" Maggie asked. It was a lovely village, she saw, with half-timbered houses on both sides of the street, and a small church on the square.

"Do you remember where the garage was?" Pete asked. The sharp click of their horses' hoofs against the cobblestones was the only sound in the silent town.

"I'm not sure. We came into town from the east, didn't we?" She pointed toward the only intersection. Lights at the corner flashed stop and go without a car in sight. "I remember that," she said.

"Let's ask," Pete said, dismounting and taking the reins of both horses.

"I'll ask at the butcher's," Maggie suggested and slipped from the chestnut mare. She had spotted a man in a white coat and apron leaning into the shop window when they went by.

As she entered the shop, the butcher was bent over the counter, and she said from the doorway, "Excuse me, sir, can you tell me where the garage is?"

He looked up and she saw that he was Arthur, the butler at Ravenshurst.

He seemed not to recognize her and only answered, "The garage, madam? It's around the corner, at the end of the street." He smiled and, picking up his knife, cut expertly into a side of beef.

Maggie backed out of the shop, not taking her eyes off him, and then she hurried back to Pete.

"The butcher is Arthur—you know, the butler. He served us drinks last night."

"It can't be, Maggie." He could see the fear again in her eyes. "Look, people in these backwater places are all related, brothers and sisters, first cousins. Everyone intermarries, and they all look alike.

Maggie glanced back at the shop. "Are you sure?" She wanted to believe him.

"I'm sure." Pete smiled. "Did he say where the garage was?"

"Yes, up the street and around the corner." She moved to take her horse from him.

"Let's leave them. We'll get our bike and find the police. The cops can take the horses back to Ravenshurst."

They tied the horses to the parking meter and

walked to the garage. It was at the end of the short street, and as deserted as the rest of the town. They walked straight through to the workshop.

"Mr. Wade?" Pete called and waited for a reply. No one answered. "It may be the off season in England," he said impatiently, "but this is ridiculous. Doesn't anyone work?"

"Let's get the bike ourselves," Maggie suggested.

In the rear of the workshop they found it, spread out on the dirt floor in the dark corner, the frame still bent, the front wheel off.

"Wade didn't do a goddamn bit of work on it. And he told me on the phone yesterday afternoon that he had the parts. He said it would only take him overnight to fix it." He shook his head. "That shit!"

"He lied just like everyone else has been lying to us." Maggie could feel the surge of fear run through her.

"Come on, let's go. Wade can have this wreck. When we get to London, I'll just file an insurance claim." Pete took her arm.

"But how will we get there? We have no car, no bike. We can't ride horseback all the way."

"That's how," Pete answered softly. They had walked back to the entrance of the shop and he had just seen Jason Mountolive's Rolls parked across the street, outside the bakery.

Maggie's eyes followed Pete's. "You mean steal it?"

"Maggie! Jason is our host. Is it stealing to drink his Scotch or use his bath towels? Of course not—so come *on*!"

They ran out of the garage and across the street, keeping the car between them and the windows of the bakery. At the side of the Rolls, they crouched down and Pete slowly opened the door and climbed into the front seat, sliding across to the righthand drive.

He reached for the ignition. "Damn. No keys!" He stopped for a moment, trying to decide what to do, then pulled out a small pocket knife and slid below the steering wheel. "Keep down," he warned Maggie, as he searched for the wiring to the starter.

"Can you do it?" she asked.

"I could when I was seventeen. Although no one in Fresno had a 1937 Rolls."

Maggie peeped over the edge of the window. She could see Harry inside the bakery. "Okay?" she asked.

"So far." He stripped the insulation off the wires and spliced them together.

Maggie looked again. The chauffeur had turned away from the counter and was walking toward the front door. "He's coming, Pete," she whispered. The baker came to the front door, too, and then she saw that he was the stable boy from Ravenshurst. This time it couldn't be a relative, or a brother. It was him. Or a twin brother. She knew that face.

Pete pulled himself up and slid behind the wheel. "Let's see if the old magic works." He touched the wires to the metal and the engine caught. Pete pumped the gas and released the brake. The car moved slowly from the curb, leaving Harry startled on the sidewalk.

Maggie looked back at the chauffeur, now running alongside. He was waving, shouting after them. Pete pressed the gas pedal to the floorboard and the car roared down the cobblestone street. Harry had stopped running. He stood with his hands on his hips and, though Pete wasn't sure, it looked as if he was smiling, watching them as they stole his master's Rolls.

At the bottom of the short hill, Pete nearly lost it. The car spun out as he turned abruptly on the wet cobblestones, but he held it on the road and they raced over a small stone bridge and out of town.

"Which way?" Maggie asked. Beyond the bridge was an intersection of three country roads.

"Left, I guess." Pete had no idea which way to turn; he knew only that Ravenshurst was behind them, on the other side of the village, and any road this way would take them away from the mansion.

He raced through the intersection, not even looking out for traffic, and took the left fork.

"I wish we had my maps," he said, down-shifting, and the Rolls fishtailed again on the wet tarmac.

"Easy, Pete, no one is following," Maggie said. But that didn't reassure him. The road behind was empty, no cars, no trucks, no one at all pursuing them. Why hadn't Harry gone to the police?, he wondered.

He raced the heavy car; he felt relieved to be away from the house, free and on his own. Only now did it begin to sink in that they had left their luggage behind on the front lawn of the mansion, and that they had lost their new Triumph. This was beginning to be an expensive trip, even if it wasn't their money.

Ahead was another junction, another cluster of roads. He slowed, then stopped to give them time to decide which way.

"Any suggestions?" he asked. The roads were nondescript, unmarked and single-laned.

"Go right," Maggie said, guessing.

Pete shifted and took off. Her guess was as good as any. He had no better idea.

This road took them up and out of the woods. They were riding the crest of a ridge, a clear, straight road across the green fields and between stone walls. Pete pressed down on the gas and the Rolls responded. He raced the car until the road left the fields and ended at the iron gates of Ravenshurst.

"I don't believe this!" he exclaimed. He wheeled the car around and pulled away, taking the first turn to the left.

"Well, now we know where we are," Maggie said. "Everything this side of the valley must be Ravenshurst property."

They were quiet now, both realizing that they were lost, caught in a maze of country lanes and unmarked roads. At each intersection Pete turned left, tried to remember if they had gone that way before, but the junctions all looked alike, the same scenery, the same stop signs. For all he knew, they were turning endlessly in circles.

The Rolls broke out of a small patch of trees and topped the hills. But all they could see at the end of the road was another set of Ravenshurst gates.

"Oh, God." Pete spun the car away from the property. "This isn't possible," he said, peeling rubber.

"Yes, it is," Maggie replied, but Pete did not hear her. Maggie slipped down in the seat. She did not believe that they would ever find their way out of this lost corner of Kent.

"We'll go back to the village," Pete suggested, "and try a completely different route." He glanced up at the sky. If he could see the sun, he could get some idea of which way he was traveling. But the sky was overcast, with winter storm clouds low on the horizon.

"Can we find the village?" Maggie asked.

"Sure. I'll just backtrack." But at the first junction he realized he could not unravel the network of crossroads and country lanes they had already taken. It would be only blind luck if they made it back to the village.

He drove wildly now, turning the Rolls impulsively from one road into another. The wheels screeched on the quick turns as he braked, then stepped on the gas. After a dozen turns and another ten miles, he drove the Rolls into a forest of trees and a thick mist.

"Oh, great! This is all we need. What a country!" He searched the dashboard for the light switch, but immediately the car was out of the mist and climbing a hill.

Pete knew instantly where they were. He had seen this stretch of land from the bedroom windows.

He let the car roll slowly to a stop. Across the lawn was the massive stone mansion of Ravenshurst.

Maggie was still slumped in the seat. For a moment she did not move. She just sat looking at the house, at the way the fog crept around the stones, rolled across the hillside and leveled the land with its white shroud. Lights were already lit in the mansion, tiny cat's eyes in the stone facade. Then she stirred and opened the car door.

"Hey, Maggie," Pete protested. "Where the hell are you going?"

She kept walking toward the house and he

pushed open his door and ran after her.

"Maggie, what's going on? We're leaving," he said, stopping her.

"I can't," she answered, looking past him toward Ravenshurst.

"What do you mean? We've just spent most of the day trying to get away. We've got a car, now let's go!" He pulled her arm, but she wouldn't move.

"I can't, Pete, and I don't think they'll let you go either. They don't want us to leave."

"No, they'd rather kill me. There have been three, four attempts on my life already. And they're trying to kill you, too. You were right about that truck." Pete moved around so that he was standing between her and the house, blocking her eye contact with Ravenshurst.

"But that doesn't matter. Jason Mountolive won't let us go."

"What do you mean?"

She nodded toward the Rolls. "Why does his car keep coming back here?"

"Because we don't have any maps, that's why. We've been driving endlessly in circles. If we had a map, I bet we'd see that all the roads lead to this house. That's very common on big English estates; they planned them that way in the Middle Ages. What we have to find is the new road, the throughway to London."

Maggie kept shaking her head. "That won't work, Pete. Let's go back inside and find out what they want with us. Maybe after that we can leave." She started walking again, but Pete grabbed her shoulders and shook her fiercely.

"Maggie, it's more than that. We meet a healthy-looking man who suddenly is dying. We go to his house and find out we're expected by five people who already know where we're from. Mountolive gives you a ring that won't come off and tells you you're written into his will." He paused a moment but she said nothing, and he squeezed her arms tightly to make her pay attention. He wasn't hurting her, but there were tears in her eyes.

"A championship swimmer drowns and two men tell you you're part of the Six, whatever the hell that means. I don't like to turn tail and run, Maggie, but believe me, I don't want to take another shower in that house. Now, come on, we're getting out of here." She still said nothing, but allowed him to propel her back to the Rolls.

"All right," he said, getting into the car, "what we have to do is make our own map. We can get back to the village from here, we know that at least, and then we'll ..." He shifted the Rolls into first and the engine died.

"Now do you believe me?" Maggie said. There were no longer tears in her eyes. She opened the door.

"Wait, Mag! I can start it." He slid down below the steering wheel and touched the wires together but this time there was no spark.

Pete sat up and stared at her, angry and frustrated by what was happening to them.

"Tell me why, Maggie," he asked, not raising his voice.

She shook her head. "I don't know yet." She seemed lost.

"Okay, then, goddamn it, let's go back and start asking some questions."

Chapter Seventeen

ADAMS WAS WAITING FOR THEM, as they had known she would be. Neither one greeted her, but as they passed by, she spoke to Maggie.

"Miss Walsh, dinner will be served in the Grand Hall at eight o'clock, if you'd like to join us."

Upstairs in their bedroom, the clothes they had left behind in the saddlebags had been cleaned and ironed and laid out on the bed. Another fire had been set in the fireplace, heating the room with its steady blaze.

"I'd like to know how they knew we'd be back." Pete stood before the fire, warming himself.

"They had it all planned," Maggie answered. She was no longer frightened. She felt as if she had walked onstage and into a play being acted out around her. There was a part for her, she knew, and she knew also, instinctively, that she was the focus of the drama, the reason they had all gathered at Ravenshurst.

There was a knock on the bedroom door and each glanced at the other. Then Pete called out, "Yes?"

"Hello—?" Barbara Kirstenburg peeped around the door, then pushed it open and came in. She was carrying several dresses over her arm.

"Where have you been?" she asked, smiling.

"Oh, just for a ride in the car. Harry let us borrow it," Pete answered, not looking at her.

She came further into the room. "Yes, Americans must find this countryside very lovely. So clean and green." Her English was sharp, the accent a mixture of French and Russian. Smiling, as if she were trying to be nice, she said to Maggie, "I thought, since you didn't bring anything formal, you might like to choose a dress for dinner."

"That's really very nice of you." Maggie moved closer to the older woman, touched by her sudden kindness. It was the first genuine friendliness any of the guests had shown her since they arrived.

"It's nothing, really." Barbara placed the gowns on the bed. "Here, pick any one." She moved back toward the door, stopping at the mirror to touch her hair, to see that it was in place.

"Barbara," Pete said, moving away from the fire, "would you tell me something?" He tried to make it sound casual, but he knew there was tension in his voice.

She looked away from the mirror, her face immediately alert, but she tried to soften her suspicion with a smile. It didn't quite work, and she studied Pete with cool, appraising eyes.

"I might," she answered. "What is your question?"

"Maggie told me last night about that ceremony up in Mountolive's room. What's it all about?"

"Oh, that!" She laughed and looked toward the mirror, studied her reflection, as if looking for something. Then she answered slowly, thoughtfully, "That's not a simple question, Pete." She paused, as if selecting the right words. "The Six who wear this ring are all beholden to Jason, that's all." She moved closer to the mirror, but now she was watching Pete in the reflection.

"I'm not beholden to him," Maggie said defiantly.

"Then why are you here?" Barbara asked.

Maggie shrugged. "We—I had a job offer, to come to London, to decorate..."

"And who gave you that job?" Barbara interrupted.

"Grandier Limited...Jason Mountolive had nothing to do with it."

Barbara smiled wryly and turned back to the mirror. "If it wasn't for Jason, Jacques Grandier wouldn't even have a London office, darling, let alone an international conglomerate. Jason brought you to England, not Jacques."

"Well, *I* wasn't brought here by Grandier or Mountolive," Pete stated.

Barbara looked at him and said slowly, "You're

right. No one expected you." She turned finally away from the mirror and looked at Maggie, speaking confidentially.

"I have known Jason Mountolive for more than twenty-five years. I love him deeply. And I trust him totally. Jason will give you such wealth. He will fulfill every whim, every fancy, every dream. He is a wonderful, wonderful man. And when he gives you gifts, I tell you: accept them, enjoy them."

She stopped speaking and stared a moment at Maggie, and then she moved forward and touched the younger woman's cheek, saying softly, her voice filled with both envy and appreciation, "You are very beautiful, Margaret. Very beautiful."

Maggie shook her head.

"No." Barbara stopped her. "Accept that compliment from one who knows rare beauty." She paused, as if deciding whether to say more, then added, "And Jason Mountolive is another who knows and appreciates it." She turned and walked to the bedroom door.

"Is that why I was selected?" Maggie called after her.

"Perhaps. He selected us all for his own reasons, and we do not know why." She spoke slowly as if remembering. "I only know that he came to me when I needed him most. He said he would make me a princess. And he did, he did. He gave me everything I wanted. And when I needed him in my life, he was always there to protect me. Like a father . . . but more than a father could ever be." She paused and looked at Maggie. "Trust Jason, darling." And then she left, closing the door behind her.

"Trust Jason—?" Pete mumbled. "Hell, I don't trust any of them, her included."

"Pete," Maggie whispered. Her hands were trembling.

He took her into his arms and held her against him. Her body trembled against his, and he held her tight, as if he were trying to squeeze the fear from her soul.

"Pete, they're trying to kill us." It was so clear to her now, so obvious.

"What do you mean?" He hadn't wanted to frighten her, but that was what he, too, believed.

"Everything that has happened . . . You in the shower . . . the misfired arrow . . . then the truck . . . They are trying to kill us, like they killed Maria."

"Who? Maria was alone when she died. We were all in the Grand Hall."

"Not all of us. Not Clive. By the time we came back from the pool, he had gone upstairs—to change clothes, Karl said. But he could have gone into the pool and murdered her."

Pete picked up the thread of her suspicion. "But it couldn't have been Clive that fired the crossbow at me; he wasn't in sight. Karl could have, though. He claims it was the cat, but he was trying to kill me . . . or even Jacques."

"But why?"

"Because of the money. If Mountolive is going to divide his estate equally among you all, then one less means they share more."

"Jason said his estate was vast, immeasurable."

"When it comes to money, you cannot have enough. Look at these people—thanks to Mountolive, they've lived like kings and queens. You heard what Barbara said: for some crazy reason of his own Mountolive has been supporting these people, making them rich and famous.

"Now Mountolive is dying. You don't think that frightens them? Christ, their whole way of life will change. The great white father is dying. It doesn't matter that his estate is 'vast and immeasurable'; they're scared shitless. Clive Jackson is just a punk. Without Jason, what is he? If he's scared, he might be willing to kill off the other inheritors to have it all for himself. And Karl I've never trusted. Those two, independently or together, are trying to get rid of *all* the others—and that means you, too."

Maggie sat down on the edge of the bed. It did make sense. What had frightened her the most—Jason's signet ring, the ceremony, the ghastly hand reaching through the plastic curtain to grab her—none of those had been the real danger. It was the others she had to fear, Clive and Karl, and perhaps even Jacques and Barbara. It was a relief, in a way, to know her enemy.

"What is it?" Pete sat down next to her, and the bed shifted with the weight of his body.

"Oh, I'm not sure. I'm just trying to think it all through." She seemed very far away from him, and he wished that he were the one Mountolive had chosen, he the one whose life was in danger. She was twisting the ring she still wore on her finger and just as he was reaching out to reassure her, she turned to him, her eyes strangely bright, and said, "Pete, would you make love to me?"

Her desire for him ran through her in quick currents. It trembled her hands as they touched his chest and slipped across his body. She needed to consume him, to caress, to kiss and hold his body, to lose herself in pleasure. Her desire was blinding, raging, and she could not control it. In his dark eyes, she saw a moment of fear. Then it passed and he allowed himself to be loved.

She raised herself to dominate him, to devour his lean body with her lips. He moved to take her into his arms and she shook her head, stopping him. This time it was her pleasure to lead, probing and provoking him until he was faint with desire. But still she would not let him touch her, and when he tried, she just brushed his hands away.

And when she was ready, she moved above him once again and their union left her gasping. She fell into his embrace and at last she allowed him to love her.

His face was against her. She could smell his hair, his body. She loved his smell, the animal heat. She moaned in his ear, ran her fingers through his hair and clutched him, loving the pain he caused. She did not resist him now, but let herself be swept along with him, carried into the deep sea of his passion and surrendering herself to his strength. All the warmth of her body rushed to her center, and she came, and he poured himself into her.

They lay quietly watching, smiling at each other. It was dark in the room, the last light of the afternoon, and the flickering fire cast shadows and silhouettes.

Maggie kept touching him, gliding her hand over his wet skin. His body was so soft, so smooth, she could not keep her hands from him. She kept looking, watching, marveling, as if she were a child and he were her favorite toy.

She waited for his eyes to close. She loved to

watch him sleep. It was not that he looked innocent, asleep, but that he seemed to enjoy it; it gave him pleasure, and she wanted him to have all the pleasure in the world.

But for herself, she was afraid to sleep, afraid that she would have another nightmare. But though she resisted, she could not keep awake, could not keep from dreaming.

The halls were lined with mirrors and she watched herself as she ran from room to room. Her hair was loose and hung to her waist, and her feet were bare beneath the long linen nightgown she wore. She felt the cold stone of the floors. And she had the child with her.

Something was wrong. Something had happened, but she did not know what. Through the windows she could smell the smoke of torches, and shadows swirled against the walls. The doors and windows needed to be bolted to keep them out, but there were too many and she was alone. The men broke inside the front door. She knew them. In the reflected lights of their oil lamps, she saw their angry faces as they searched for her. Then they spotted her up above, her white gown flashing in the dim light, and, shouting, they came after her, up the wooden staircase, their boots crashing on the steps.

She reached the bedroom and slammed the door behind her, throwing the bolt before they could grab her. It was their bedroom; she recognized the fireplace and the canopy bed. But it was lit by candles, and the man in the bed was not Pete, though he had Pete's dark looks, his mustache and dark hair. She could see the fear on his face and it enraged her.

They were hitting the door, over and over, a hideous sound, like the world breaking apart. She hugged the boy to her breast and ran to the windows. The shadows were everywhere around her, she could not escape.

She turned and shouted at him to help, but he lay weeping on the bed. She hated him, hated him for his cowardice, hated the others for their ignorance and envy. She would make them all pay, she swore, and then the door gave way and they were upon her.

Maggie woke abruptly, wrenched from her deep sleep in the quiet house. She sat up, sweating under the heavy blankets, and looked around the room, still lit by the soft glow of the fire. Her scalp was damp with sweat, and she threw off the heavy blanket so she could feel less oppressed by its weight.

She closed her eyes and bits and pieces of the nightmare came back to her. She was afraid to sleep, afraid of what she might dream, and she lay awake and listened to the strange sounds of the old mansion.

Chapter Eighteen

"MR. JACKSON?" THE NURSE found Clive alone in the game room. She stood in the doorway, an impeccable white figure. "Mr. Mountolive wishes to see you." There was no hint of request in her voice, no humility. At Ravenshurst, Adams' word was law and guests were expected to treat her with respect.

But not Clive Jackson. He hated the woman whom he called the White Bitch.

"Thanks, luv," he replied, as he stepped away from the table and replaced his cue in the rack. Even from across the game room, he could see her body tense. Familiarity such as his was not tolerated.

She was, after all, Mountolive's private nurse. She was the one who kept him alive, and it was that boundless attention and care that Clive bitterly resented. Let Mountolive die. Divide the fortune and let each of them go his own way. He was tired of the last-minute summonses to Ravenshurst, sick of the tedious weekend house parties.

"And how's the old man this afternoon, Adams?" Clive asked as they climbed the back stairs. He had hoped she would bristle at his irreverence, but she only answered evenly, "He's fine, Mr. Jackson."

"What do you think, Adams? Will he live the weekend?"

"I don't know, sir." She paused only long enough to add coolly, "He might very well live longer than any of us." Then she opened the door and let Clive into the room.

"Clive—?" The old man's voice was weak and rasping now.

"Yes, sir." Adams had insisted that Clive stand outside the glass partition. He could not see Jason, but he did not really want to. Maggie Walsh had fainted at the sight, and he was not tempted to prove he was tougher.

"Clive?" Each word came slowly, painfully, punctuated by the hideous rasping. It was as if the old man's lung was gashed and he was losing breath with every syllable.

Clive's hands began to tremble. It wasn't possible that Jason had heard about the episode in Key West. But then Jason always knew about his adventures, even before they happened.

"I've warned you before about your appetites. You want it all, don't you, Clive?" Hearing the disappointment in the dying voice, Clive realized his own privileged position was in jeopardy.

"I'm sorry, Jason." Clive bowed his head in total submission to Jason's will.

For a moment there was silence except for the tortured breathing, then Jason went on: "But I did not call you here to . . . lecture. I called you, Clive, to say good-bye."

Clive jerked his head up and stared through the glass at the shadowy figure behind the curtain. Tears sprang to his eyes as he accepted the fact that his benefactor was dying. No longer would there be Jason Mountolive at Ravenshurst to support and protect him.

"Good-bye, sir." Tears flowed down his cheeks as he turned toward the door for the last time.

Adams dimmed the lights, casting Jason into shadows, and stood back to let Clive pass. When he was gone and the door shut, Jason called Adams to him for her instructions.

The lavish buffet was spread on the long oak table of the Grand Hall. The household staff had spent the long afternoon and early evening cooking the dozens of dishes and decorating the table with gold candle holders, the finest Ravenshurst china and silverware, flower arrangements and baskets of fresh fruit.

At eight o'clock, when Adams came to inspect the preparations, everything was in perfect order. Nodding her approval to Arthur, she instructed him to call in the guests.

"Yes, ma'am." Arthur slipped on his white gloves

and left for the library, where three of the guests had gathered for drinks.

"I don't understand." Barbara spoke angrily to Jacques, then turned to Karl, who sat alone on the sofa, away from the other two. "We have been together for so long, and suddenly, on what is perhaps the last weekend of Jason's life, we are presented with someone new—and told she is one of us." She downed her champagne without pleasure.

"But Barbara, you know there must be six!" Jacques insisted. "What do you think has kept Jason alive all these years? He has been searching for the Sixth."

"But there are no longer six," she shouted. "Have you already forgotten Maria?"

"Six *were* present at Ravenshurst at the same time," Jacques answered. "That is the requirement set forth in the book. Here, I'll refresh your memory." Setting his drink aside, he strode to the library shelf and scanned the books. Suddenly he gasped in alarm. "It's missing," he shouted.

"Is this what you're looking for?" Karl asked, pulling an antique volume from the breast pocket of his suit. He held the book out to Jacques and for an instant they exchanged uneasy glances. "You were right, Jacques," Karl added, "I should have read this years ago." In the dim light of the library he seemed tired. "It would have better prepared me for this... how do you say?... this fateful weekend?" He shrugged and sipped his drink in resignation.

"I've read that!" Barbara announced, "It's nothing but myths. A ghost story."

"But we are part of the story, Barbara." Jacques

spoke softly as he carefully turned the pages of the book.

"I'm certainly not." She was pacing the room, too nervous to sit.

Karl raised his eyebrows. "Not part of it? Just what sort of agreement did you make with Jason?"

Barbara stared at him, then answered sharply, "That's none of your business."

"Ah!" He smiled sardonically, including them both in his response. "We all have made our private arrangements with Jason, my dear. We are together, all for one, one for all."

"And what about Maria?" she demanded. "Wasn't she one of us?"

"Yes." He nodded, drifting off into his own thoughts. "Yes, of course, of course..." He looked across the library, eyes blurry and unfocused, still frightened by the sudden death, so unexplained, so close to him.

"Here it is," Jacques interrupted, looking up from the book. He held the page toward the light and read:

"'...And when the six seal bearers shall be assembled, there shall be selected one among them to carry forward...'"

"And what is that supposed to mean?" Barbara demanded, irritated by the implication of strange secret oaths. She had promised Jason obedience when he had taken her out of the misery of Latvia, but she had given her word freely. She owed him everything, her life, her fortune, her body and her soul. But there was no secret pact. She was proud of her allegiance.

Karl rose. Without asking, he took the book

from Jacques and slipped it back into his pocket. Then he turned to Barbara. "What all that means, Fraulein, is that one of us will be selected to carry Jason's legacy into the next generation, as it has been carried forward from the time of Margaret herself."

"But Jason told us last night we would all share equally in his estate." She frowned, shaken by the suggestion that her wealth and power might disappear with Jason's death. She continued looking at Karl, as if she expected an explanation from him, but it was Jacques who answered her.

"Yes, Barbara. But . . ." he paused, torturing her with his silence, then added, "We came to Ravenshurst this week as Six. The Six Seal-bearers." He glanced at his signet ring. "Now there are five. Will tomorrow find only four of us to share the wealth of Ravenshurst?"

"And if so, which four? And which of them will bear the legacy into the future? And will Jason be the one to decide? Has he already selected one of us? Is it you, Karl? You seem preoccupied this evening. Does the prospect of that vast wealth and power unsettle you?" Jacques looked next to Barbara and smiled, "Or is it you? In Margaret's book it is written that woman is the devil's decoy."

Barbara backed away. "I know nothing of such foolishness!"

"Perhaps you are the one, Jacques." Karl looked up from lighting a cigarette.

"Perhaps." Jacques nodded. "Or Clive, whom Jason thinks of as his son."

It was then the library door opened and Arthur stepped inside to announce that dinner was served.

* * *

Jacques was the first to see Maggie as they left the library. He whispered to the others to look up as she moved toward the staircase on the second floor. At the top of the stairs she paused and looked down, taking them in with a sweeping glance.

She was dressed in a black, elegant gown, cut square at the neck and flowing down over her body. She wore no makeup, but had worked her hair into braids and pinned them into a crown. She looked elegant, even regal.

At the bottom of the stairs, Karl, pale with shock, exclaimed, "It's Margaret . . . Margaret of Walsingham."

"Uncanny!" Jacques whispered. Then, recovering himself, he said coolly, "Now who do you think is the true descendant?"

Karl grabbed the Frenchman's arm. "I won't allow her," Karl stammered. "It's too ridiculous . . . the fortune and power . . . passing to a giddy young girl . . ." His eyes followed her as she turned to greet Pete, who was wearing freshly laundered blue jeans tucked into his boots.

"Such a handsome couple, don't you think?" Jacques' words were tinged with a sarcasm intended to provoke Karl, but Barbara cut him off. "Look, she's coming down."

Followed by Pete, Maggie slowly descended the stairs, smiling at the others. Her assignment was to gain their confidence without letting on she knew someone was trying to kill her.

"Why, aren't you lovely?" Barbara exclaimed, approaching Maggie and taking her hand. "The gown looks superb, my dear." She smiled, but her eyes were cold and unresponsive as she turned to Pete. "Tell me, why don't you marry this beautiful girl?"

"She hasn't asked me yet." Pete smiled back, then took Barbara by the arm and led her toward the Grand Hall.

"May we?" Jacques asked Maggie as he and Karl approached.

"My pleasure," she smiled graciously at them both. Looking beautiful gave her confidence. She turned toward the open double doors of the Grand Hall and slipped an arm into theirs, one man on either side.

"When are you leaving?" she asked casually.

"Tomorrow, early," Karl said.

"In the helicopter?"

"Of course."

"Very impressive."

"Yes," Jacques said, "very impressive. But that's the way Karl operates. He knows how to create an impression. Like you, Margaret." His manner was cool, but his voice was hard.

"Isn't this lovely?" Disregarding Jacques' comment, Maggie exclaimed over the food and flowers.

"Well, what's all this?" Clive asked, dashing into the room and up to the buffet. He was wearing a white shirt and vest, but no tie or jacket. He had showered so recently that his hair was still damp.

"Good evening, luv," he said to Maggie absently, not bothering to look up from an examination of the food. He couldn't recall when he had been so hungry.

The food, he supposed, was compensation for

the fear he had experienced at Jason's bedside. It had been a close call which he had survived with only a scolding, but the encounter had drained him. It cheered him to think that soon he would not have any such worries. Soon Jason would be dead.

"Give me a bit of that ham, would you, luv?" he asked Maggie, holding out his plate.

Maggie served him a few slices and then they moved down the table, helping themselves to stuffed artichokes, salad, stuffed mushrooms, pâté, baked potatoes, thin slices of veal and hot biscuits.

"Chicken, miss?" the butler asked, as Maggie approached him.

"No, thank you, Arthur. I haven't any room on this dish." She laughed at the mammoth amount of food on her plate. She hadn't eaten all day and the sight of the luxurious spread was making her ravenous.

"Some chicken, Mr. Jackson?" Arthur asked.

"No, thanks, Arthur, my man." He held up his equally brimming plate. "Let me hack away at this for a while."

Maggie walked to the sofa to join Jacques, who was gorging himself on two plates of food. He was clearly a glutton, and watching him eat was repulsive, but she had questions to ask. Their lives, Pete had warned, depended on what she could learn at the dinner.

She toyed with her food, then bent toward Jacques and said confidentially, "You know the conversation we were having yesterday just before Maria..."

"Of course." Jacques paused, his knife and fork

poised over his plate. His face was red from the excitement and the warm fire and his lips were moist.

Maggie hastily scanned the room to make sure no one was listening. "Can we continue?"

"Naturally." He set the knife and fork down, then wiped his lips with his napkin.

"I was just wondering," she began nervously, "if you people are involved in..." She played with her food, then went on, "...if you people are involved with black magic, you know, with the occult..."

Jacques smiled, "If you want to call it that."

"So are you, luv." Clive had come up behind them, and she glanced up, angry to discover that he had so blatantly eavesdropped.

"Don't get uptight." Clive laughed, misreading Maggie's look. "You have to look at it as just another way of life." He kept grinning, coughing a bit as he laughed. "I mean, we don't ride around on broomsticks or anything. We use helicopters and Rolls-Royces! Quite nice, really." He coughed again and set his plate of food down on the end table.

Jacques looked angrily at Clive, then spoke quietly to Maggie. "Clive likes to treat everything with the same shallow humor. But, I must tell you, it is a serious matter. The Power is not granted indiscriminately."

"Just what is this Power?" Maggie persisted.

"Oh, Jacques is so pompous," Clive coughed as he tried to answer. "Forget why there is a Power and enjoy it." He couldn't stop, and his face was turning red from the exertion. "Here's where it's at," he wheezed. "The old guy's gonna die." He coughed again, loudly, painfully squeezing out the words.

"And we're here to bury..." Suddenly he gasped, clutching at his throat, then went reeling back and stumbled to the floor.

Maggie cried out and jumped up, spilling her plate in the process. "Pete!" she shouted, but he was already at Clive's side, kneeling next to him.

"I...can't breathe..." Clive choked out.

Pete looked up and yelled to Arthur, "Get Adams.... Hurry!" Then he spoke calmly to Clive. "Can you swallow?"

Clive could only gasp. Pete slipped his finger into Clive's mouth and deep into his throat, feeling for a piece of food that might have lodged in the windpipe. Clive's face was turning purple and his eyes bulged; they stared wildly at Pete.

Adams rushed into the room and the others backed away to give her access to Clive.

"Clear the table," she directed, kneeling next to him. "Make a space to stretch him out." She glanced at Pete and said, "Help me."

Once they had lifted Clive onto the table, she took a fork and pressed the handle against his tongue. "How long has he been like this?" she demanded.

"I don't know, thirty seconds. A minute. It just happened," Pete explained. "We were eating and he started to cough. I didn't pay attention at first, but then he began to gasp."

"It's all right," she answered calmly. "We have time. Three or four minutes, at least. I'm sure it's a bone. We will have to perform a tracheotomy."

"My God, no!" Pete objected. "You'll kill him."

"He'll die for sure if I don't do something." Adams turned to Jacques. "That knife, please." She pointed to the long meat knife, which Jacques handed her, avoiding the others' glances as he did.

Maggie backed away from the table, her eyes locked in on Clive. He was past gasping now, and his lips were purple from lack of oxygen.

"What I am doing is necessary," Adams told them. "I am going to make a simple insertion into the neck over the trachea and below the Adam's apple. This will allow air to reach the lungs, bypassing the laryngeal obstruction." She turned to Pete and instructed, "Hold his arm." As she cut into Clive's neck, he shrieked in pain.

"No, no!" Maggie turned away and ran stumbling from the Grand Hall.

"Adams, stop! Please!" Barbara begged, but the nurse kept cutting as blood spewed out in a fine warm mist. It sprayed the front of Adams' dress, flooded Clive's throat, and spilled onto the table.

His body jerked as he tried to stop her, but Pete fought to keep him still. Then Clive gasped again and the blood bubbled out of the hole in his neck. His legs jerked violently for a moment on the hard wooden table, the boots hitting the wood like a drumroll. For a brief instant his whole body shook under Pete's grasp. And then he lay still.

"He's dead," Barbara whispered, dazed by the suddenness of it.

Pete released his grip on Clive and stood back. He stared down at him, then picked up a napkin and tried to wipe the warm blood off his hands and shirt. "You'd better get the police back here," he ordered Adams.

"I will, Mr. Danner." Adams placed the bloody kitchen knife by Clive's body.

"And this time I want to see them," Pete added, raising his voice.

Adams was examining the incision in Clive's neck. Holding the flesh apart with one hand, she stuck her fingers into his windpipe and pulled out the bloody splinter of a chicken bone.

"This was stuck in his throat." She held it up, showing it to them all, Clive's blood still dripping from her hands. "He had only four minutes to live."

"You going to call the police or do you want me to do it?" Pete shouted.

Adams paused, stared at Pete and then said quietly, "Mr. Danner, why don't you go to your room? You're very overwrought. I will take care of everything."

"You've taken care of enough," Pete shouted back. Then he bent over and, picking the white table cloth up off the floor, drew it over the body of Clive Jackson, the second of the six to die in the house of Jason Mountolive.

Chapter Nineteen

MAGGIE FLED THE GRAND HALL, afraid to go to her bedroom alone. Instead she headed for the fire-lit library, a warm and cozy room, close enough to Pete to call him if she needed help.

She immediately switched on every lamp, bathing the room in light. Yet even with all the lamps shining, the library was haunted by shadows. The whole house seemed haunted, even the whole of England, and she suddenly missed the sunny openness of California.

Walking to the fireplace, she heaved more logs on the flame. The dry wood caught quickly, and in a few minutes the fire blazed so intensely that she had to step away from the heat.

It was then that she noticed the portrait of the young woman. The girl was Maggie's age, dressed in the same square-necked black gown, with the same long brown hair swept up off her neck and fastened with a gold headpiece set with pearls. She wore only two pieces of jewelry, a heavy lavaliere around her neck and the signet ring of Ravenshurst. In her hands she clutched a thin, leather-bound book.

"She's quite beautiful, isn't she?" Karl's voice startled her. She hadn't noticed when he'd slipped into the library and stood watching her studying the portrait.

Maggie was too stunned to answer him. Seeing her likeness in the sixteenth-century portrait was eerie but exciting, like discovering an unknown twin.

"Do you admire the ring on her finger?" the German persisted. He moved closer, dragging his bad leg across the thick carpet. Maggie could hear him approach, his shuffling step driving a wedge of fear through her. She had to force herself to keep from screaming for Pete.

Too frightened to turn, she could feel him close behind her, could hear his heavy breathing and smell his breath, rancid with tobacco and whiskey.

He spoke softly in her ear, as if telling her a filthy story. "She lived here. When she was just your age, she was dragged from this house and burned at the stake by order of Queen Elizabeth the First. Her name was Margaret, too—Margaret Walsingham."

Maggie flinched and spun around to Karl. Her eyes widened and she stared at him.

"My mother's name was Walsingham," she cried without thinking. But then it was too late. Too late to heed Pete's warning not to tell these people anything which could be used against her.

Karl looked up at the portrait and continued. "This Margaret Walsingham was succeeded by her illegitimate son, who inherited all her wealth and power. And so it has been ever since, as prescribed in a book she wrote—called *The Legacy*."

He slipped the small leather-bound book from his suit pocket and pressed it into her hands, closing her fingers around it.

"I want you to read this, so you will fully understand what has been happening here." He glanced at the door, to make sure no one could hear them, then said, "I heard you ask Jacques if our group is involved with the...the occult..."

Maggie looked intently at the German. "Well, is it?" She held up the book that Karl had just given her. "And while we're at it, just what is the legacy...?"

Karl looked again toward the library door, then whispered, "You *must* read Margaret's book. It will explain the inexplicable happenings at Ravenshurst. You will learn the meaning of Maria's death."

"It was an accident..."

Karl shook his head. "Expert swimmers like Maria do not hit their heads on the bottom of pools."

"Clive killed her, didn't he?" Maggie asked bluntly.

Again Karl shook his head. "Then why is Clive now dead? Tell me, Margaret, what did he eat this evening?"

She thought a moment. "Ham, for sure, and some pâté. His plate was full. I think he took mostly vegetables..."

"Any chicken?"

"No. I remember. When Arthur asked him, he said he had too much food on his plate."

"Well, he choked on a chicken bone," Karl replied. "Adams pulled a splinter from his throat."

"Oh, God." She could still see Clive stretched out on the table, gasping for breath, his legs jerking up and kicking the table as he tried to stay alive. "But that's not possible," she protested. "He didn't eat any chicken."

"It happened nevertheless, Margaret." He gestured toward the book clutched in her hands and urged, "Read that and you'll understand. Remember, too, who your only friend is at Ravenshurst."

But it was not Karl who was her friend. Of everyone at Ravenshurst, only Pete could be trusted. She backed awkwardly away, mumbling, "Excuse me...I must..." Then she turned and rushed from the library, desperate to find Pete.

Karl watched her go and allowed himself the luxury of a small, tight smile. He had played that very nicely. Very nicely, indeed. He went to the bar and poured himself a brandy. He had not eaten anything; not after seeing what Adams had done to Clive. But he continued to drink, despite the fact that the liquor would dull him when he most needed to be alert.

Jacques was the killer, Karl was sure of that. Sly, insidious Jacques with his fine manners and soft voice. The French gentleman. The connoisseur. Karl snorted. The bloody murderer. It had to be Jacques and Adams working together. The proper, condescending Nurse Adams. Another killer in their midst.

He could still see her cold-bloodedly cutting Clive's throat. And the blood. Quart after quart of hot, hissing blood pouring from the incision. Karl could still smell it, taste it, and he quickly gulped the brandy to wash the taste away.

Jacques and Adams had worked it all out. One final weekend when they would kill off everyone else Jason had written into his will. Maria and Clive already were gone, and those who survived would be attacked one by one, like sheep singled out by wolves.

That had been their plan. Quite smart. Karl snorted again, amused.

Jacques had been the one who told him to read Margaret Walsingham's diary, page by page. He agreed with Barbara that it was all nonsense, a book of lies and superstitions. Jacques and his talk of the occult! Jacques would have them believe the devil was among them. Karl smiled as he sipped his brandy.

Let Jacques believe that Karl Liebknecht, survivor of the Hitler Youth Corps, the Western Front, and the terrible years of the Occupation, was frightened of ghosts and devils. It served his purposes perfectly to have all the others believe that. Just as it had been a master stroke to convince Maggie Walsh that she was a true descendant of Margaret Walsingham. Tomorrow morning, when the helicopter landed on the lawn, he would be the only one waiting.

He strolled over to the fireplace, warming himself as he watched the beautiful gold vermilion of the flames. The Americans would have to die. Especially the young man, who was already pressing for an investigation. With any luck, Jacques or Adams would handle that problem for him.

Karl stared at the fire as he made his decision. If Jacques did not eliminate the Americans, then he would have to do it. He already knew he was not afraid to kill. It would not inconvenience him if, before the weekend was over, it was necessary to kill again.

The fire was dying. Karl leaned over and threw another log onto the blaze. The fire hissed and a small log tumbled forward onto the firestone. Karl lifted it and sent it back with the tongs. For a moment, he stayed crouched before the flames, enjoying the perverse thrill of the intense burning. He was thinking of Jason. The old man had hung onto life longer than he was useful, and as Karl was damning him for living, the fire struck him.

The flame bellowed out of the hearth in a rolling cloud of heat. It licked his bare skin, blinded his eyes, and burned his lips and tongue as if a searing poker had been jammed between his teeth. His shriek of pain caught in his throat and he fell back onto the floor, the flames following, covering his body like a blanket.

The fire burned his clothes first. It reduced his shoes to warped rubber, melted his watch, his fine jewelry. The gold cigarette case burst open and the ink in his fountain pen shriveled away in the tube.

He did not lose consciousness immediately. He felt the white flame envelop his body and burn away his eyebrows and silvery hair. He heard his own skin crackle like grease on a skillet as the flame ran up his sleeves to his armpits and burned a path across his chest. He felt the flame as it spread over his body, seizing his soft genitals and then burning down the length of his thighs. He was dead before the fire began to roast his remains.

He burned for ten minutes. The fire did not spread; it consumed only the body of Karl Liebknecht, leaving the library untouched. His body curled, shrinking like a log on the hearth, as his limbs jerked and contracted and finally broke off from his trunk like dried, rotten branches.

The smell of burnt flesh was intense, but that, too, was contained within the room, not even spreading when Adams opened the door and stepped inside, locking it behind her until her work was done.

By now the charred remains were only a small lump, blackened and unrecognizable. The fine silvery hair was gone, the elegant features obliterated, the rangy body reduced to a compact heap which smoldered like a charcoal pit.

Adams paused to study the charred mass. The sight itself did not upset her, but the thick smoke and the dense odor made her eyes water. She blinked rapidly as she went about her work, opening the windows to clear away the smell and the smoke. Then, emptying the wood from the iron bucket, she took up the tongs and meticulously collected the remains, stacking them like peat. It took her only one heavy load to clean Karl Liebknecht's corpse from the library of Ravenshurst.

Chapter Twenty

IN THE SAFETY OF their bedroom, Pete and Maggie sat close together on the bed and examined the leather book, turning the ancient pages carefully, Pete reading out loud bits and pieces of the sixteenth-century script.

"'And they came for me unto this house. I heard noises on the lawn outside, shoutings and cries, and I left my darling, the lord of my heart...

"'I got up and went to look, to see what was the cause. It was just dusk, a long, lovely summer dusk. I could feel the breeze off the sea, the late summer breeze...

"'I went downstairs into the new house. The house had been finished only the year before by my husband James, and then James was killed in a hunting accident . . .'"

Pete flipped through several pages and continued, his quiet voice filling the room as he read,

"'I was in such a state with the house and farm, my lover would ride up in the late afternoon from the village to comfort me. I was so young then, not yet twenty, and not meant by God for such dealings . . .

"'Yes, I tell you all, I loved him. And he wanted me as well. I could not stand the pain he was suffering, and he told me God would forgive us.

"'. . . And then the child, my bastard child . . . I named him after my love . . .'"

"Don't read any more, Pete," Maggie suddenly insisted. She tried to take the book from his hands, but he pulled it aside.

"Look, Karl told you to read this, didn't he? Okay, we're going to find out exactly what these people are doing, what kind of black magic this is." He opened the book again and continued.

"'. . . I stood in front of the house and I saw the villagers and farmers coming for me, crossing the fields below the lawns, moving swiftly, their shouts and cries carrying to me on the summer wind. It was dark now and their lights looked like hundreds of tiny fireflies.

"'I knew what had happened, and that they were coming for me. I could not see their faces, they were still only at the stream below the meadow, but the smell of their hatred was on the night air and I bolted the doors and ran from room to room closing windows.'"

Pete flipped through several more thick pages and picked up the ancient account.

"'... They dragged me from the house and tied me to a tree in the meadow below the barns and they stripped my body. They would not allow me that decency. Then the women whipped me until my skin broke and drew flies and mosquitos from the marshland. They left me to die in my own vomit and blood.'"

"Please, Pete, stop," Maggie begged, pacing the bedroom, but Pete would not stop; he had to find out for himself what had happened to Margaret Walsingham.

"'... I was unconscious for a time and only lived because some servants came out of hiding in the woods and cut me from the stake and carried me to the house. We found my poor babe left for dead in the doorway, his small back branded with the letter "B."'"

"'... Upstairs in my marriage bed we found my lover. He had cut his own throat and bled to death like a pig. His face was white and his mouth gasping. The summer heat had dried the blood and the room smelled already of his decay. The flies were like a cloud of dust around his head.

"'I loathed the sight of him. I had thought he was my lover, but he was not. He was one of *them*, those common people who sin in secret and damn others. And from that moment, I made my own pact with Satan.'"

Pete stopped reading and sighed, then tossed the book on the bed. "This book is crap, Maggie: How do they expect anyone to believe all that?"

"I do," Maggie answered slowly, but Pete did not hear her. She walked to the bed and carefully picked up the book. She could not expect him to understand. He had not dreamed the nightmares, nor felt the heavy weight of the Ravenshurst ring.

She opened the book and silently read from the last pages of the sixteenth-century diary. "'I, Margaret Walsingham, do bear witness in this wise: Take whatever thou desirest, saith the Lord Satan. For thou shalt be my welcome debtor, and thou shalt pay thy debts to me in later time. For I shall press thee to my service in the Halls of Darkness...'"

"Did Karl say he would help you?" Pete asked.

Maggie nodded, but her mind was preoccupied. It was there in the small book, the long, tragic tale of the Englishwoman who had fallen in love and committed her life and soul to the service of the devil. Maggie read the painful pages, experiencing the terrible truth of the woman's story. In dreams and nightmares, in sudden, strange flashes of recognition, she was reliving the anguish of Margaret Walsingham. When would she relive the triumph?

But Pete was persistent. "Let's see if we can get a lift on his chopper tomorrow," he was saying. "We can't drive out of this goddamned countryside, then we'll fly over it." He took Maggie by the arm and together they went to the library to find Karl Liebknecht.

Adams lugged the firewood bucket through the passageway and out to the yard where Arthur met her. "Not yet," she instructed as she handed him the iron pail. "Wait for the others to retire for the night." Then she returned to the library, built up the fire again and closed the windows. Finally, as Jason had willed, she unlocked the drawers, removed the files, and placed them on the desk. Adams made sure they were open and in easy sight before she slipped out of the room.

Maggie and Pete hurried into the library, only to find it empty.

"He was here a few minutes ago," Maggie protested.

"Damn! He must have gone to sleep, although I don't know how. Every time I close my eyes I see Clive."

"Please, Pete, stop." The image of Clive's death throes still made her shiver, and she moved closer to the fire to warm herself. Then she saw Karl's half-filled brandy glass. "Look at this—I bet he hasn't gone up yet. Let's give him a few minutes; he could be in the bathroom."

"Do you want a drink?" Pete asked, from the bar.

"Yes, I need something. I can't get warm." She wrapped her arms around herself and rubbed her upper arms. "There must be a window open." She went to check.

It was as she stepped away from the windows that Maggie noticed the files on the desk. She paused, her eye catching sight of the newspaper clipping with the headline ITALIAN SWIM CHAMP IN ROME VICE SCANDAL. She picked it up and saw a younger Maria Gabrielli, smiling as she stepped out of a swimming pool.

"Pete, look at this!" She held up the clipping.

"What?" He was bringing Maggie her vodka-and-tonic when the library door opened and Adams stepped inside.

"Is there anything you require before bed, Miss Walsh?" she asked, looking past Pete to Maggie.

"No, thank you, Miss Adams." Maggie managed a smile.

"I've got a question," Pete interrupted. He handed Maggie her drink, then turned to the nurse. "Where's Karl?"

"He had urgent business in Munich," Adams replied, moving briskly toward the door.

"But I was just talking with him!" Maggie protested. "How could he have left so quickly?"

"The maid packed for him," Adams explained, "and Harry drove him in Mr. Mountolive's car." She already had her hand on the door.

"Now wait!" Pete demanded, but the nurse, as if she had not heard him, proceeded through the door, closing it behind her.

Pete slammed down his drink, sloshing whiskey onto the table. "Goddamn it! I'm getting tired of these people disappearing on me. I'll be right back." At the door, he glanced back at Maggie. "Lock it, will you? I don't want to come back and find you missing too." Then he was out in the foyer, searching for Adams.

"No, Pete, don't leave me!" She ran to catch him, but the foyer and staircase were already empty. There was only the white cat, running silently up the stairs to the second floor. Reluctantly, she went back to the library and locked the door behind her.

But the confinement did not comfort her. The room suddenly seemed to grow darker, more menacing. Again, she moved from lamp to lamp, trying to dispel the shadows cast by the thick drapes, the heavy leather furniture.

As if in a bright spotlight, the portrait of Margaret Walsingham shone among the shadows, drawing Maggie to it. It was astonishing. The Walsingham genes had survived intact over so many generations and created a mirror-image. She could almost *be* Margaret Walsingham. It defied all the laws of heredity.

Wind from the open window ruffled the papers on the desk. She picked them up and began to read the yellowed clippings about Maria Gabrielli. There were more stories of Maria's other arrests in Rome, accompanied by photos of her emerging from court. And with her, every time, holding her by the arm and directing her through the crowds of reporters, was Jason Mountolive.

Maggie quickly picked up all the papers and began to scan them. There were clippings on Karl, Clive, Barbara—all the guests of Jason Mountolive except Jacques and herself. She brought the files over to a leather armchair near the fire, knowing she had more reading to do. Maybe these would help her to understand the reason for this strange weekend. She needed to know the truth to stay alive, even though this knowledge was drawing her deeper into the secrets of Ravenshurst.

She had to discover her own role in this play and, while she waited for Pete to return, Maggie read all the files that had been prepared for her.

Chapter Twenty-one

PETE DID NOT FIND Adams in any of the downstairs rooms, and as he went through the dark kitchen he decided to check for himself whether the Rolls had been driven at all that night. He let himself out the back door of the kitchen and walked across the stable yard to the garage.

The wind had blown away that afternoon's clouds and cleared the sky. He could see the path by the full, bright winter moon. It was a clear, cold night and the sharp evening air stung his hands and ears. He had come outside wearing just a sweater over a shirt.

At the garage doors, he stopped and listened for voices, but the yard was quiet. Then he bent down and lifted up the garage doors, sliding them back. The Rolls was parked inside, its headlights facing the door. Pete raised the hood and tentatively touched the engine block. It was cold. The car hadn't been driven in hours, certainly not since they had raced it around the countryside.

"Munich, my ass," he whispered and lowered the hood. Karl hadn't left. So why had Adams lied to them? What had happened to the man? Adams, certainly, wouldn't tell him. It pissed him off that she barely acknowledged his existence. Maggie was the one she addressed, never him, and always with that smirk. Just once before they left Ravenshurst, he'd like to slap it off her face.

Pete ducked outside the garage and pulled the door shut. But when he turned the corner to walk back to the kitchen, he saw a man's shadow at the cellar door. Backing up against the garage, he watched the person stagger across the yard, weighed down by the large bucket he carried. Pete could not make out who it was, though the man came within yards of the garage door, his leather boots stamping on the cobblestones as he walked.

Pressed into the shadows near the door, Pete watched the dark figure leave the courtyard through a small wooden gate and continue away from the house, toward a cluster of outbuildings.

When the man was out of hearing, Pete followed him, keeping close to the stone walls, then to the trees, as he crossed the fields to the barns.

The outbuildings formed three sides of a quadrangle, enclosing another cobblestone yard. A set of iron gates made up the fourth side. Closing the gates behind him, the man continued out into the middle of the courtyard. Pete waited until he had vanished before leaving the trees and sprinting to the corner of the building.

As he paused to get his breath, Pete noticed that the winter moon was shining like a spotlight exactly where he stood. He was captured like a black and white photograph in the brightness of the moon and he had to move before he was sighted. Careful not to awaken the animals, he crept along the length of the building toward the gates and then stopped, hidden behind a water trough.

Pete heard the man stop also. Heard the iron bucket being set down roughly on the cobblestones. He looked up carefully over the edge of the trough. The man was standing a dozen yards from him, floodlit by the moon. It was Arthur, the butler, and now he was dumping the contents of the bucket onto the cobblestones. The top of the iron pail clanged as it hit the stone and the noise echoed in the country silence.

Taking the bucket with him, Arthur disappeared into the barn at the far end of the quadrangle. Pete stayed there a few minutes more, waiting for Arthur to return, or for lights to be turned on inside the barn, but nothing happened.

Why was Arthur disposing of garbage in the barnyard at midnight?

Now the night was still, except for the dogs. Pete could hear them moving inside the barn. Occasionally one of them growled, the deep-throated rumble of a sleeping animal being disturbed. Pete stood up and looked around. Arthur had not come back. Now was the time to risk it.

Silently, he swung open the gate, then closed it

carefully behind him and walked quietly over to the heap of garbage.

Within ten yards, he could smell it. The reek of charred flesh puzzled him, and it wasn't until he crouched down beside the heap that he saw the dismembered left hand of a human. The blackened fingers sticking out of the pile were twisted grotesquely where the skin had shrunk and pulled the joints out of shape. Still on the charcoaled hand he saw the Ravenshurst ring, tarnished by the fire and unrecognizable except for its shape. As the full meaning of what he was looking at struck him, Pete recoiled. The terrible smell filled his whole head, as if he could almost taste the remains of the corpse of the German.

He would need the ring as evidence for Maggie and the police! He touched the scorched hand tentatively, then grasped the ring and pulled hard. The finger broke off, snapping like the leg of a wishbone, and Pete stumbled back, his stomach revolting against what he was seeing and what he had done. Then the dogs were upon him.

The wire doors spanned back and one after another, the Dobermans attacked, frenzied by the smell of flesh.

As the first dog sprang, Pete could see a flash of sharp white teeth in the moonlight. He raised his arm and caught the dog across the chest, sending it reeling away. The dog yelped with pain. Another seized Pete's ankle, digging its teeth into his leather boot. Pete tried to yank his leg away, but the dog was persistent, bracing its front legs to tear off Pete's foot as if it were a chunk of meat. Pete kicked at the Doberman with his free leg and caught it in the head. Immediately, the dog's grip slackened and gave way.

There were more dogs then; racing from the cages and barking wildly in their rage. They rushed past Pete, knocking him over, as they scrambled for the charred remains of Karl Liebknecht. If Arthur had let the dogs loose, Pete reasoned, he would be back. Pete rolled away from the ravishing pack and stumbled to his feet. Then he was running for his life.

He did not stop to open the gate, but swung his body over the top iron rail and landed safely on the other side. Across the fields he ran, back toward Ravenshurst, the huge mansion now silhouetted against the night sky of Kent.

Chapter Twenty-two

EVEN IN THE LIBRARY, Maggie could hear the dogs, but she had lost all awareness of her surroundings, absorbed as she was in the clippings. At first the rapping at the window sounded like a bare branch hitting the glass. Then she knew it was someone watching her. She could feel it.

Someone was behind her in the room who was going to kill her. She was next on the list. She did not look up, but sat staring at the pages, the print blurring before her eyes. Strangely, she felt only relief. At least it would be over. Then the realization hit her: "Oh, God, I'm going to die. Pete has left me and I'm going to die."

The window rattled again. Someone was trying to get into the house. She spun around and saw a dark face pressed against the glass, motioning to her.

And then she saw it was Pete; he was signaling her to be quiet. She yanked open the window and helped him inside, keeping as quiet as possible. The night air was freezing cold, but his shirt was damp with sweat, and he shivered in her arms when she held him.

"Sweetheart, what happened?" she whispered, her arms wrapped about him, trying to warm his body.

"Christ, Maggie, they killed him! They burned him to a crisp and fed him to the dogs." His teeth were chattering from cold, exhaustion, and his own horror at what he had seen.

"Who? What do you mean?"

"Karl," he whispered. "They killed him. Burned him to death and now, down at the barns, they fed the remains to the Dobermans." He slumped in the leather chair and she knelt beside him, still clinging to his body. She would not let go as he told her the whole story, of the Rolls parked in the garage, of Arthur with the iron bucket, and of the unleashed dogs attacking him in the barnyard.

Because she had not seen it, she had great difficulty believing it.

"Are you sure, Pete?" she asked when he finished. "Couldn't it just have been burnt meat? Something spoiled in the kitchen?"

He took the charred ring from his pocket and held it up. She too fell silent. It was the twin of the one she wore, and it could only have come from

Karl's finger. Then she remembered what the clippings had told about Karl, and she understood. His death had not been an accident or a random killing. It had been deliberate, and the execution ritualistic.

Maggie went to the desk, brought back the files and spread them out before Pete on the rug.

"I started looking through these after you left," she explained. "Look at the one on Maria. It's a news story about a prostitute who worked for her. The woman was killed in some Italian millionaire's pool. She died mysteriously, the paper said. See! Here's a photo of Maria surrounded by paparazzi, and if you look closely at the background..." she held the photo toward the light, "...there's Jason Mountolive getting out of that car after her."

She gave Pete the stories to read and picked up the next file. "All these are about Clive. In the early '70's he was promoting a small band." She pulled a clipping from the pile. "According to this account, the drummer of that group was mainlining heroin and choked to death on his vomit. Clive was busted for supplying the smack, but he got off because the guy who fingered him changed his story. The case never got to trial. And look who's at Clive's side during it all."

She handed Pete the clipping, which showed Clive in a local pub after the charges had been dropped.

"Mountolive," he whispered. In the shadows at the edge of the photo was a smiling Jason, out of place among the long-haired singers and their fans.

"There's more." Maggie went on. "Here's a newspaper story on Karl. The headline reads,

'Arson Suspect Acquitted in Courtroom Drama,' and again Jason is with him. See him here? Thirteen years ago, an employee of Karl's was burned to death in an ammunition-factory fire. Karl was accused because the factory was open illegally in Germany. He was acquitted, and Jason was there."

Pete took the files and flipped through them.

"You see what's happening?" Maggie said.

"Sure. They've all been killed in an identical way. Maria by drowning; Clive by choking to death; and now Karl in fire. The punishment sure fits the crime."

"And somehow Mountolive was involved with them all. He helped them get free, and they, in turn, owed their allegiance to him. As Barbara was telling us upstairs..."

"What about Barbara?" Pete interrupted.

"There's only one clipping. She was involved in the stabbing of a society hostess in France, the wife of a publisher." Maggie searched the file and came up with the clipping. It was a photo and text article from *Paris-Match* dated 1959. "Not much to it—the woman was stabbed with an ice pick. The murderer was never found, and a scandal developed because Barbara was rumored to be involved with the woman. But there was no police investigation."

"And Jacques? What did he do, rape little girls?" Pete asked.

Maggie shook her head. "There's nothing in these files on him or me."

"Where did you find them anyway?" Pete asked, shuffling through the clippings.

"On the desk." She pointed across the room. "Somebody left them out."

"They weren't left, Maggie," Pete said quietly. "They were put there on purpose so you would find them."

"But by whom?"

"By Jacques Grandier."

Pete was calm enough to start thinking through the series of murders. Maggie had been wrong about Clive; he wasn't the killer. Jacques was. Jacques with his smooth French manner. It was Jacques who was skillfully disposing of the others whom Mountolive had selected for the legacy.

"Jacques wanted you to know about the others," Pete explained. "I'm sure there's a file on him as well. He must have some connection with this group of killers."

"Then why me? I've never killed anyone." There was panic in Maggie's voice. She was suddenly afraid Pete would think she had hidden something from him.

"I know, darling." He reached out and for a few moments they just held each other. They felt safe within each other's arms. Maggie blocked from her mind the knowledge that someone in the huge old mansion was waiting to end her life. She squeezed Pete tight until he said, "We have to warn Barbara. She'll be next."

"How do you know? Maybe the next one will be me."

"Because she's alone. That's how Jacques has managed to kill everyone else. He isolates people and strikes when they're alone. We might even be too late already." He grabbed Maggie's hand and they ran from the library and up the staircase, shouting, "Barbara! Barbara!"

Chapter Twenty-three

"WHICH ROOM IS HERS?" Pete asked, as they reached the second floor.

"I don't know."

"Okay, let's try them all." He moved across the hall and knocked on the first door, shouting Barbara's name, then opening it. "Stay with me," he ordered Maggie. "We've got to stay together from now on."

Before they reached the bedroom at the far end of the hall, the door opened and Barbara stepped out into the passage.

"What is it?" she demanded, pulling her silk kimono on over her nightgown. "What time is it? What is wrong with you people?"

"Oh, Barbara, thank God." Maggie went to her side. "Thank God, you're all right."

"All right? What do you mean?" She stared at both of them.

"It's Karl," Pete began.

"Karl?"

"He's dead," Maggie whispered.

"Oh, God, no!" She grabbed Maggie's arm. "Not Karl, too."

Maggie was trying to explain. "Pete found...found his body. He had been..." She couldn't tell the woman.

"Someone has been playing 'kill the guests,'" Pete spoke up, "and we think it's Jacques."

But Barbara was not listening. Dazed, she pulled away from Maggie and turned back into the bedroom, murmuring, "Three of us now..." Her hand was pressed against her forehead, and she stumbled and almost fell.

Pete caught her by the arms and settled her on the bed.

"I don't believe you," she whispered, tears in her eyes. "I must see him! I must see Karl!"

Pete knelt down beside Barbara, took her hands into his and said quietly, "Barbara, it isn't possible." Her hands were freezing.

She stared at him, and even through the tears Pete saw that she did not trust him. He would have to tell her everything; otherwise she would never believe.

"Jacques burned Karl to death. I'm not sure how, or with whose help, but I saw Arthur feed his remains to a pack of dogs down at the barns. I took his signet ring as evidence."

He tried to show it to Barbara, but she slapped his face.

"Stop it!" she shouted and then convulsed into sobs. "I can't believe that. It's crazy, crazy. . . . Jason would never let this happen to *me*. Never!"

"Jason is old, Barbara," Pete answered, still kneeling beside her. "He can't protect you any longer. Jacques is out to kill everyone who has a share of the legacy. Now this means you and Maggie."

"But why?" She stared at Pete, her face red and lined with the tears that had streaked her makeup and made her look old.

"Because of the money," he said firmly.

"My God, there's enough for us all, more than enough. Jason never denied us anything. He supported our businesses, our silly whims, anything at all."

"Jason is dying, Barbara, and his fortune will be divided among you. For some people, that isn't enough. Jacques wants it all and he's willing to kill for it. He wants all of the Ravenshurst legacy."

Barbara nodded blankly. She had to see Jason. He would tell her what to do, but she knew Adams would not let anyone disturb him.

"All right," she said, "what do you want me to do?"

"Come with us. We'll get Harry to drive us straight to London tonight, and tomorrow we'll get in touch with Jason and contact Scotland Yard. We can't defend ourselves against Jacques, not here at Ravenshurst, and not tonight."

She nodded. Without answering, she picked up the telephone by the bed.

"Hello?" she said softly, speaking into the phone. "Give me the chauffeur, please... What? Because I'm leaving Ravenshurst, that's why," she snapped. She looked at Pete and Maggie. "Jason's staff has become so rude. When I was much younger, Jason told me that he'd make me a Russian princess. And in many ways he has. But now he is leaving us and his staff knows it. Why couldn't it last?" She had begun to cry again. "Why couldn't it last forever?"

She recovered and said into the mouthpiece, "Hello? Harry? Yes, I wish to leave at once. Miss Walsh and Mr. Danner will be leaving as well." She paused again, listening. "Yes," she added, "London. We'll be ready in ten minutes. Please have someone come for our luggage." She hung up. "Ten minutes," she announced.

"The last time Harry said he'd take us to town, he left without us. Let's hurry." Pete looked toward Maggie and said, "I'll get the saddlebags. Okay?" He had left the bedroom before she could answer.

"I'll be packed in a few minutes," Barbara said, as she stood. She was desperate to get out of the mansion. She began to babble to Maggie, about the wonderful weekends at Ravenshurst when Jason was younger, but Maggie wasn't listening. When Pete had left her, the fear had returned. She was terrified that Jacques would kill both her and Barbara while they were still alone.

"I'm getting Pete," Maggie called to her. "He shouldn't leave us."

She turned, ran out of the bedroom and back down the hall, panic spreading through her body. The door to their bedroom was open and lamps were burning inside. A patch of their light shone on the hall carpet, but when she ran into the room, Pete was gone.

"Pete?" she shouted. The saddlebags were still on the chair, but their clothes were packed. She knew then that they had done something to Peter. Something terrible had happened to him and now she was alone against Jacques.

As she ran toward the door to rejoin Barbara, Jacques stepped out of the dark hallway and blocked her way. In his blue-velvet dinner jacket, fear shining in his eyes, he didn't look like a killer.

"Margaret, I must speak with you." He was trembling.

Then she saw the shotgun. He could swing the shotgun in a short arc, less than ninety degrees, and kill her. She was already within six feet of him. It would be impossible for him to miss. But then she saw that he was only using the gun to motion her into the room.

He was whispering something, too, that she couldn't follow, something about the others, about what Pete was doing. Her Pete. Suddenly she realized that she was no longer afraid. All her fears had disappeared when she saw that Jacques was afraid of her.

"Let me by, Jacques," she demanded. "Let me out of this room."

"But you must listen to me, Margaret. We need each other." He was shaking; his face was flushed and soaked with sweat. "He'll kill us otherwise."

"Who will, Jacques?" she asked calmly.

"Danner! Your lover. He's going to kill us all." Jacques was so choked with fear, he could hardly speak.

For just a moment the wild accusation made her hesitate. For two days she had lived a nightmare where reality and truth had been painfully altered, as if by some supernatural force: the murders, the dreams, the portrait, the Rolls turning repeatedly back to Ravenshurst. There was no explaining such things away. But she knew Pete. She loved him and he loved her. She almost laughed at Jacques' attempt to drive a wedge between them.

"No, Jacques, it isn't Pete who is killing your friends," she answered, walking toward him, certain of her power over him. He backed away as she approached, stepping out into the hall. "You are the murderer and we know that."

He was shaking his head wildly.

"You can't kill us all, Jacques. Pete and I are leaving and we're taking Barbara with us. The legacy will never be yours alone."

"But it isn't me, Margaret," he pleaded. "I didn't kill them." The shotgun hung loose in his hand as she brushed past him.

"It isn't Pete," she answered as she left him in the dark hallway.

"No," he whispered. "It isn't Pete. It's you, Margaret."

"What? What are you talking about?"

"You're the one who is killing us all." She was shaking her head, misunderstanding what he meant, but he continued, his voice rising as he spoke. "You don't realize it yet, but the Power is with you. He gave it to you, and it is you who has been destroying us."

"You're crazy, Jacques."

"But I won't let you kill me," he shouted, backing

away from Maggie. He raised the shotgun and leveled it at her.

"Jacques, you don't understand." She spoke calmly. The man's paranoia was out of control but, for some reason, she still did not fear him.

"Don't come near me!" he shouted, backing away. His hands were shaking, but he kept the shotgun leveled at her.

He pulled the trigger of the double barrel. The shotgun blast roared in the silent house and he turned and ran, ran through the Portrait Hall, into the old wing of the house and upstairs onto the roof.

The pattern of buckshot had gouged a tight three-foot hole in the wall behind her. It had shattered a mirror, cut a table lamp in half, peppered the wood-paneled wall with pellets and destroyed an upholstered wingback chair, but miraculously, it had missed Maggie. At point-blank range, Jacques had missed her, as if she hadn't even been standing in the hall.

Barbara ran out of her bedroom and shouted down the length of the hallway, "Margaret, what was that? What happened?"

"It's all right, Barbara. It was Jacques, but he's gone. Hurry! We've got to leave. I'm going downstairs to find Pete." Leaving Barbara in the hall, Maggie ran toward the staircase.

Barbara closed the bedroom door behind her, then quickly threw the rest of her clothes into a suitcase, leaving out only her traveling outfit. She slipped from her silk kimono and, as she folded it into her suitcase, she caught the reflection of her body in the full-length mirror. She moved closer, running her open hand across her breasts and down her naked body. She had a fine figure. She was not aging, and she had kept herself trim and taut. Smiling, she turned sideways. She was tightening her buttocks when the glass mirror exploded outward, sending thin slivers of glass flying at her face and body, cutting into her soft fair skin with a hundred swift incisions. The flying glass sliced her face, dug into her shoulders and breasts, and pierced her heart, shredding her skin the length of her nude body. Then the thin slivers of glass flew back to the frame, as if drawn by a magnet, and recomposed themselves into a solid, unmarked sheet of glass.

Barbara was dead before she fell back onto the deep white rug of her bedroom. Her dying heart kept pumping blood through the severed arteries and deep gashes, and she lay in the warm, moist blood like a fish cast into stagnant water, another dead guest of Jason Mountolive.

Chapter Twenty-four

MAGGIE FOUND PETER IN the downstairs hall, coming back in from outside. Through the open front door she could see the Rolls parked in the driveway, its engine running and the lights turned on. Already the darkness of night was softening, and she could see daylight breaking low on the horizon. What had happened to the night?, she thought, and then said to Pete, angry that he had left her alone, "Where did you go?"

"To make sure Harry got his instructions right. At least he does what Barbara tells him. I was afraid he'd disappear on us. Where's Barbara?"

"Packing. I came to find you." She slid into his arms and hugged him silently. "Jacques found me," she said, clinging to Pete. "He tried to kill me just a few minutes ago. He said I was the cause of everyone dying." She was in tears now, and she gushed out everything that had happened to her in the few minutes they had been separated.

"He should have killed me, Pete," Maggie insisted. "He was less than six feet away from me. Why did he miss?"

"I don't know. It might've been anything. He obviously didn't want to kill you. Maybe you're too important to him alive." He poured her a glass of Scotch and made her swallow some.

"No," she answered, shaking her head. "He wanted to. I saw that in his eyes."

"Don't worry. We'll be out of here in ten minutes. I promise." He tried to sound positive as he wrapped his arm around her shoulder and hugged her to him for a moment.

"We've been leaving Ravenshurst since we first arrived, and we haven't made it yet," she answered. She couldn't stop thinking of what Jacques had told her. She knew it didn't make any sense. She hadn't even been in the rooms when Maria, Clive and Karl had died. Still . . . She was going to ask Pete what he thought when the drop of blood plopped into her drink, dissolving into the Scotch. Then another drop hit her hand like a large, single drop of rain. And suddenly more blood was falling on Pete, dropping onto his arms and hand. Both of them looked up to see the wide red stain spreading slowly across the ceiling. Instantly, they knew what it was.

"Oh, Christ!" Pete exclaimed, and ran. Maggie ran with him, out of the library and upstairs to Barbara's bedroom. Outside the closed door, Pete held Maggie back, saying, "Don't go in. Let me see how bad this is."

She nodded and stood to one side as Pete opened the door.

He saw her bare feet first, then her long legs, the naked body and the pool of blood beneath.

"Don't look," he called out to Maggie. He was leaning against the door frame. The sight of Barbara was worse, somehow, than the burned body of Karl.

"I *must* see," Maggie said.

Pete shook his head. "There's nothing we can do." He tried to close the door, tried to stop Maggie from looking at the bloody corpse, to keep himself from seeing the naked dead body.

"I have to see," Maggie insisted, and pushed by him, staring into the brightly lit bedroom. It was such a lovely room, Maggie thought irrelevantly, beautifully decorated in soft pastel colors, with a fireplace, antique furniture, an elegant bed, and the standing full-length mirror.

Maggie moved cautiously further into the room and stood over Barbara's corpse, staring down at the body, hideously punished.

"It *is* me," she whispered.

"What do you mean?" Pete came closer to her.

"I was the last one to see her. I was the last one to see Karl..."

"Maggie, don't." He touched her arm, realizing what was happening to her.

"And Maria," she went on, "and Clive at supper. It's me, I tell you."

"Mag, stop!" Pete moved in front of her, blocking the view of Barbara, and seized her by the shoulders. "Stop it!" he demanded, angry that she

was letting herself become obsessed by Jacques'
accusation.

"It is, Pete, it *is*, it—"

He hit her across the face and her body shook,
then trembled in his arms. He pulled her close to
him and hugged her. "Honey, it's this place. It's
gotten to you, that's all." He kept her tightly against
him and buried her head in his shoulder. "It's gotten
to us both. You know it's Jacques, you can see that
he's done it. Now let's get him before he gets us
both."

He took her by the hand and led her out of the
room. He would have liked to put her to bed, give
her a Valium and let her get some sleep—she'd be all
right once she had a chance to sleep—but he
couldn't leave her alone while he searched the
mansion for Jacques. It was too risky. Together
they had a chance to get away, but only if he could
kill Jacques. The man was crazy. The killings of the
others were premeditated and brutal. He and
Maggie couldn't expect less if Jacques cornered
them in the house.

In the doorway he stopped and looked out,
glancing both ways. The second-floor landing was
empty and still dark, lit only by the other bedrooms
that cast patches of light on the hall rug.

"We want to make it downstairs to that
anteroom, you know?, where we found all those
guns," Pete instructed. Then he moved into the hall,
keeping back against the wall as he led Maggie
down the curving staircase to the entrance hallway.

Downstairs the foyer was empty and the door to
the anteroom open. They ran across the foyer and
into the room, closing the door behind them. The

door to the gun cabinet had been left open and Pete took out a shotgun, then searched the drawers for shells.

"Damn!" He slammed drawers. "No shells." He replaced the shotgun and glanced around the room, searching for something else to use.

"Is this any good?" Maggie picked up the crossbow. "Do you know how to shoot it?"

"No, but I can learn." He took the crossbow and examined the firing devices. Then he picked up a short arrow, fitted it in the slot, and pulled back the bow. "Christ, that's hard. The trouble is that Jacques has a shotgun. I can't get close enough with this bow, even if I knew how to shoot it."

"Don't try it, then," Maggie cautioned.

"I have to, Mag. We'll be damn lucky to get out of this place alive, and we're only going to do that by taking some chances. Now I want to get outside of this building. He's got too many rooms and dark corners to hide in. Outside, we can move around and make him come to us." Pete opened the anteroom door and looked out.

"Where do we go?" Maggie asked.

"Behind the Rolls." Pete looked back upstairs. There was no one on the second-floor landing. He could hear no one moving. Only the white cat raced down the staircase, running wildly through the house from room to room.

They moved toward the front door and Pete opened it. The Rolls was still parked in the driveway. The engine had been turned off and Harry was nowhere in sight. "Run to the other side of the car, Mag," Pete directed. "He might be watching the Rolls, waiting to see if we'd make a break for it. Get to the other side and keep the car between us and the house. Okay?"

She nodded, but did not look reassured.

"Follow me," Pete said. He crouched down and ran toward the car.

They had almost reached the Rolls when Jacques fired at them. The blast missed Pete by several feet, only flattening the rear tire of the car.

They thrust their bodies forward, tumbling across the wet grass and rolling behind the car. Jacques fired again, but this time he aimed too high and the buckshot sprayed the rear window, breaking the glass.

"Where is he?" Maggie asked, lying flat behind the car.

"On the roof, I think." Pete pulled himself up and peeped over the hood. He saw Jacques move, scrambling from behind a chimney to cross a ridge of the roof. Pete picked up the crossbow. Bracing it against the hood, he aimed and fired. The arrow ripped out of the bow and reached the high roof, but missed Jacques' body by a dozen yards.

"I'll have to get close to use this," Pete said, fitting another arrow into the bow.

"No, Pete, forget him. Let's just get away from here."

"We can't, the tire is shot out. And if we ran away, he'd only follow and track us down. He won't let us live. He needs to kill you to claim the legacy, and if he doesn't do it at Ravenshurst, then it will be in London or L.A. It won't matter where you go or where you try to hide. He has to kill you."

The tone of Pete's voice chilled Maggie far more than the cold morning air. She knew he was right.

They couldn't just walk away from Ravenshurst.

"What do we do, then?" she asked, accepting the inevitable.

He outlined a plan:

"Go to the end of the car and throw stones toward the hall windows. I want to make some noise to distract his attention; I'm going to run in the house, right under where he's standing. He won't be able to see me and maybe I can get a shot at him."

"Pete, it's not possible!"

"Maybe not, but it's still the only chance we've got. Go ahead." He kissed her quickly, as if for good luck, and crawled toward the front of the Rolls.

It took Maggie several tries before she hit the glass windows of the front hall. The stones bouncing off the panes of glass finally caught Jacques' attention. Pete saw him try to look, to find out what they were doing. Then he moved his position again on the roof, crawling toward the edge, and Pete made his break for the house.

Jacques spotted him before Pete was clear of the Rolls and swung his shotgun around. He was stretched out on the roof, holding the gun in an awkward position, and he fired in panic. The buckshot pattern caught Pete in his left leg and he fell forward once more onto the grass, clutching his leg as he tumbled.

"Peter!" Maggie screamed, and came around the huge car, running toward him.

"No, Maggie! Go back!" Pete shouted, but she kept running toward him on the lawn.

On the roof, Jacques stood up, broke open the chamber of the double-barrel, and slipped two more shells into the shotgun. Then he raised the gun and aimed at Maggie as she ran across the grass to her lover.

She was such an easy target, out in the open and within fifty feet of him, yet he hesitated, savoring the pleasure. In a moment she would be dead, destroyed, and he would be free to claim the legacy for his own.

"Margaret," he shouted. He would make her see her own death coming.

She stopped running and stared up at him, standing silhouetted against the pale, early morning sky. She stood quite still, watching him, as if daring Jacques to shoot, enraged at what he had done to Pete, at what he was planning to do to her. What a fool he was to think he could keep her from her legacy!

Jacques raised the shotgun and found her in the sight. He smiled at the pleasure her death would bring him, at all the wealth and power it meant; then he squeezed the trigger, slowly, so as not to jerk the shotgun and miss, not realizing that the barrels of the shotgun were both blocked solid with metal, as if they had never been bored.

The gun exploded in his face, threw him back onto the roof where he tumbled over one edge and rolled down toward the skylight of the pool room, crashed through the roof and fell into the water with a shower of glass. He was dead before he hit the water. The last guest was gone.

Chapter Twenty-five

MARGARET WALSH WATCHED JACQUES DIE. Saw how the gun inexplicably exploded, watched the body roll down the roof and crash into the swimming-pool skylight. Then she knelt down beside Pete and looked at his leg. The gunshot wound was not serious; no bones were broken. Only his flesh had been torn by the pellets.

"I must go to Jason, now," she said, standing again. He would be expecting her, now that the last of them was gone.

"No, Mag," Pete protested and tried to sit up. He had to stop her. But she had turned toward the mansion.

"Maggie! No! Come back! Don't go in there!" he

shouted after her and tried again to stand, but he was still too weak and he fell forward again on the wet grass.

Margaret walked across the lawn, back into the house, then through the foyer and up the curving staircase. She walked quickly, sure of herself and what she had to do. At the top of the stairs, she turned and went into the Portrait Hall, past all the ancestors, and through the door leading to the old wing. At the top of those steps Adams met her, and opened the bedroom door to let Margaret into his room.

"Thank you, Adams," Margaret said softly, and walked toward the glass partition.

"Margaret...are you there...?" The old man struggled to speak.

She kept on walking, through the glass door and into the intensive-care section of the room, moving carefully past all the life-support systems.

"Jacques is dead," Margaret reported, standing close to the bed. She could see only the shadow of the figure behind the plastic curtain.

The old man laughed painfully, and then he said, "Jacques saw in you the killer. And he was correct. The Walsingham blood proved stronger than the greed of those other pretenders. It always has been. It always will be."

"Jason, my Jason...." He was finally dying, Maggie realized, and she reached out and pulled back the plastic curtain.

She did not flinch, nor was she repulsed by the sight. Jason Mountolive was ancient, a creature from the valley of lepers, with the cancerous skin and skeleton of a corrupt soul.

His white hair was fine and thin and shoulder-length. It spread across the white pillow like cobwebs. His right eye was cataracted. Milky film clouded the pupil, and pus dripped from the eyelid. The other was sightless and without color. It stared up at Margaret like a fish eye. His skin had yellowed and was stretched across his skull, pale and translucent except where the cancerous sores had festered and the bluest ulcers formed growths the size of handballs under his chin and down the length of his throat. His decaying body smelled as if it had been dredged from swampland.

"Jason," Margaret whispered, embracing him. He had been born into her arms and now he was dying there. Her hazel eyes were full of tears as she looked at him lovingly.

He spoke once more, his voice less than a whisper, each word formed by an effort of his will. "I have been so lonely for you, Margaret," he sighed. "If only we could rule Ravenshurst together, as we did before. But the Lord Lucifer has been kind, allowing me to look on you once more.

"I knew you would come again, to take from my hands what is yours eternally. I pass them to you now, this house, this land of Ravenshurst, as you passed them once to me, when I was nothing but a boy."

He tried to go on. His lips parted but the words would not come. He no longer had the breath or the life to continue as the master of Ravenshurst. Margaret glanced at the machines surrounding him and saw the moving pens hesitate and stop. She picked up the crippled hand of Jason, the hand that had so frightened her at first with its long curling fingernails, its dry skin and fragile fingers, and kissed the signet ring of Ravenshurst. Then she stood and nodded to Adams. The nurse turned from the glass partition and left the bedroom as Margaret knelt down on both knees beside the hospital bed.

On the lawn of Ravenshurst Pete pulled himself to his feet and, using the crossbow as a support, hobbled to the front door. He knew where she had gone and he painfully climbed the staircase to the second floor, heading for the old wing of the sixteenth-century mansion.

Adams stopped him at the top of the stairs, outside Mountolive's bedroom. "You can't come in just yet, sir," she said, blocking his way.

"The hell I can't. Get out of my way, bitch!" He grabbed the stout woman by the shoulder and tried to push her aside, but Adams shoved him back against the wall, and he stumbled on the stairs, his injured leg going out from under him.

Then the nurse came after him, her fingernails going for his eyes as she hissed and jumped forward. Pete ducked his head and dove at her, catching the nurse in the middle of her body. Raising her up, he dumped her over his shoulder and down the stairs. She tumbled down the steps and hit her head against the wooden banister, landing sprawled at the bottom of the stairs, blood gushing out of her mouth, her face smashed against the railing.

Pete did not look back. He was at the head of the stairs now and he burst into the bedroom, stumbling forward into the strange hospital room. He could see Maggie, kneeling next to the bed, her face pressed against the withered hand of Mountolive.

He shouted at her to get away, to get out of the room. Then he charged forward, swinging his hands wildly as he began to rip the room apart, knocking over the machinery, tearing down the tubing, using the crossbow to smash all the screens of the electronic instruments.

He pushed over the oxygen tank and it rolled against the fuse box, which short-circuited. There was a barrage of sparks and flames, and fire caught hold of the plastic curtain. Suddenly the bed flamed up in a brilliant flash of light, engulfing the old man.

Pete grabbed Maggie and pulled her away from the bed and out of the intensive-care room. They watched the flame consume the corpse.

"It's all over, Maggie," he said, exhausted from his struggle as they watched the flame burn out. He pulled her into his arms and she embraced him, wrapping her arms around his body. "It's all right now," he whispered, holding her.

"Yes, I know," she replied and pulled from his arms and looked at him a moment. There was no longer fear in her eyes. She understood what had been done, and what she had to do next. It had been left to her. "Come," she ordered Pete, and walked out of the room, knowing that he would follow.

She walked ahead of him, down the stairs toward the center of the house. At the bottom landing she stopped to pick up the white cat that lay whimpering on the stairs. She stroked its back until the cat stirred and recovered from the fall. Then she went on to the Portrait Hall.

The household staff had assembled. They were

lined up in uniform, the old cook, Harry, Arthur, the stable boy and gardener, the servants of Ravenshurst.

"Good morning," she said sweetly to them all. The white cat jumped from her arms and landed on the wooden floor, then ran silently across the room, slipped between the curtains and disappeared.

"Hey, Maggie." Pete tried to get her attention.

The curtain flipped open immediately and Adams came into the room. She was dressed as always in an immaculate white uniform and she smiled as she greeted Maggie.

"Good morning, Adams."

"Hey, Mag." Pete grabbed her arm again and held on to her, but he kept staring at Adams, seeing her as she had been before, unconscious at the bottom of the stairs, her life's blood pouring from her mouth.

"Just a minute, Pete," Margaret said softly, and then to the others: "Thank you, Adams. Thank you, everyone, for what you have done. For all your help. It will not go unrewarded." She turned to Pete and said sweetly, "Let's go outside, dear."

And they walked together through the Portrait Hall, downstairs to the foyer and out into the daylight. The sun was up now, and the mist had burned off the lawns. It was warm as they walked away from the house.

"I don't know what to say," Pete said, as he began to understand what had happened, to realize that he had lost Maggie forever. He stopped walking and shook his head, saying only, "I've got to get out of here." He turned and limped toward the driveway.

"I have no choice, Pete," she called after him, "and I want you to stay. I need you."

He paused and turned, moving awkwardly on his bad leg. "For what?" he asked as she walked toward him.

"I love you, Pete," she whispered.

She stood directly before him now, but for a moment they did not touch. He was staring at her, looking into her eyes to see if that was true. She did not try to hide her love. It was all in her eyes, like a gift that he could accept and cherish. Then she opened her hand and, to seal her love, held up the silver signet ring.

"Trust me, Peter," she whispered, looking at him, holding him with her eyes.

"But, Mag..." He kept on shaking his head.

She stepped closer to him. "You will understand, my darling. Once you accept my ring you'll understand why it had to be this way."

He tried to pull away, but she held his hands too tightly.

"I'm not one of you, Mag. I'm not a Walsingham."

She smiled at his innocence. "It doesn't matter, Pete. I have chosen you—that's all that matters." She took his left hand and slowly slipped the Ravenshurst ring on his finger. Looking solemnly into his eyes, she married him to her fate.

He was smiling and she smiled back, happy that he had stayed with her, the first of her six seal-bearers.

"Okay," he said, sighing, "we'll give it a try." He kissed her lightly on the lips.

She began to tell him how they could use the power of Ravenshurst to remain young lovers forever, to expand their fortune throughout the world, to live always in comfort and luxury.

And he was listening; she could always make him listen to her.